The Unlucky Seven

A GIL YATES PRIVATE INVESTIGATOR NOVEL
By Alistair Boyle

Allen A. Knoll, Publishers
Santa Barbara, CA

Library of Congress Cataloging-in-Publication Data

Boyle, Alistair.
    The unlucky seven : A Gil Yates private investigator novel / by Alistair Boyle. --1st ed.
       p. cm.
    ISBN 1-888310-77-4 (alk. paper)
    1. private investigators--California--Fiction. 2. California--Fiction. I. Title.
    PS3552.0917U55 1997
    813'.54--dc21
                                        96-51686
                                          CIP

Text typeface is ITC Galliard, 11 point
Printed on 60-pound Lakewood white, acid free paper
Case bound with Kivar 9, Smyth Sewn

Also by Alistair Boyle

The Missing Link
The Con

Acknowledgements

With thanks to Richard Ney for his
software industry expertise
—A.B.

I was putzing my palms and cycads at the moment Harold Mattlock was plugging into my telephone company-provided message system.

He was one of the richest, most powerful men in the world, and that, believe it or not, was what prompted him to call personally.

And he had the grace to add to his message, "You have been highly recommended."

The only thing was, I knew what he wanted. It was in all the papers, on all the news shows, and I knew that it was the challenge of a lifetime. He wanted something I would never dream of doing in my humdrum life as Malvin Stark, beleaguered property manager. But as Gil Yates, private eye—well, things almost as strange have happened.

In my real world as Malvin Stark you might look on me as somewhat henpecked—or perhaps more accurately, dinosaur-pecked because I refer to my lungy, glass-blowing wife as Tyranny Rex. I considered calling her Bigfoot at one time, but there is some doubt of the existence of Bigfoot. Dinosaurs are a fact of life. I should know, I live with one. Besides, her feet aren't that big. Her lungs are her focal points. They put you in mind of a boombox at full volume.

Her family boasts a tradition of in-your-face over-bearingness. I work for her father. Have since our wedding day, and I don't mind telling you I've hated every minute of it.

So I am relieved to have the respite from the Wemples—Tyranny and Daddy Pimple—which I gained quite by accident. You might say it was a Walter Mitty dream world, or a Superman complex. I don't care, I am experiencing a roundish object or having a sphere or balling the wax, clichés are not my forte. My hope is to get the sense of them if not the exact words. I *do* so love clichés. Their mastery is somehow foreign to my intellect. There is a French phrase for what I do to clichés—*prop de mal* or something.

Garbled clichés are one thing fabulous Gil Yates has in common with the meek, mild Malvin. Otherwise: no comparison. From henpecked husband and harassed employee (non-sexual) to master of the universe and king of all I survey with women dropping at my feet. I tell you there is nothing like it. But I am ahead of my story.

The voice of Harold Mattlock on my answering apparatus did not sound proud or powerful, as well it might have. He was not petulant having to talk to a machine, as well he might have been. It was rather a matter-of-fact message, delivered with an accent owing its origins to the British Isles and the tone was that of a low rumble, like the sounds of a distant, monotonous sea.

A few years back, for a lark, I told a guy at a Palm Society meeting I was a private investigator. That indiscretion led to me looking down the barrel of a gun in the hand of none other than that extraordinary arms dealer, (Sing Sing class of '93) Michael Hadaad. I'm still baffled how I got out of that one alive. But it also led to a quarter-of-a-million-dollar fee. And yet, that guy who tried to give me an unsolicited nose job "recommended" me for my second job which didn't turn out so well.

No doubt I could write my own ticket with Harold Mattlock, but what were the chances of hunting down a mad bomber who got it in his head that seven people ruled the world and said the world would be better off without them? A guy who sets out systematically (and quite effectively) to kill the unlucky seven with bombs he mailed from God knows where. Three so far. Four left.

This terror has been going on for years; the bomber takes his time. Harold Mattlock is on the list. Could be next. I come highly recommended. But finding a missing daughter is one thing, tracking an art forgery is another; but going after a psychotic bomber was so far out of my league you couldn't get there from here.

Crazies are the toughest targets. You can't get a bead on them. They don't exhibit logic. It's like trying to throw a dart at a Mexican jumping bean.

My first inspiration was to not call Mattlock back. But that would have been rude. Besides, he might need help finding a daughter someday, and I'm experienced at that.

So I called, and was I astonished at the royal treatment I got. From the big man himself (in the top seven by some reckonings). He was knocking himself out just to make my acquaintance. No commitments, just a little chat. He would fly out to see me and send a limo for me—all at my convenience. Yes, he had many commitments, but there wasn't one he wouldn't change for me.

Could you say no to that?

I didn't either. Except I told him to skip the limo. I didn't want anyone to know where I hung out. One look at Tyranny Rex, the wife, or Daddybucks Wemple, the father-in-law/boss, that slab of flab, and, goosewise, I'd be cooked.

My palm and cycad garden, tract-house size in Torrance, California was the ideal venue for meditation.

Perhaps the main reason I keep at this high-stakes, higher-risk endeavor is the funds it sometimes provides to buy these rare and exotic cycads. These plants, I am somewhat ashamed to admit, can sell for thousands of dollars— and that is not a plant you need a crane to move; that is, rather, a plant that comes up to your navel, if you aren't too tall.

Fortunately, my wife, Tyranny Rex, and my father-in-law, Daddybucks, don't know cycads from daisies so they don't have to wonder where I get the dough to pay for them. So here I was, gazing at the fuzzy leaves of my rare *Encephalartos heenanii* trying to formulate a plan for bowing out of this bombing job gracefully. I did not intend to be the person to screen all the incoming packages.

The more I thought about it; the more I knew I wanted no part of this case. I didn't see how my appearance would be improved any if my nose wound up in Istanbul and my ears in Timbuktu.

Certainly I was flattered to be called by this important mogul, who had newspapers, magazines, television networks, radio stations and book publishers wherever English was spoken or remembered.

But could a level-headed person such as myself be expected to be bowled over by flattery and ignore the wisdom of experience to risk his life at the bidding of a mega-rich mogul?

Apparently.

In the tattered taxi tooling up Pacific Coast Highway, I realized everybody has his price; and with the very rich, it was a fatal mistakes to sell yourself too cheaply. It's no secret I lost a bundle on my last case. Ever since my first cavalier offer to get paid only if I produced, I have been given cause to regret it. Even when I fulfill the contract, I have to worry about getting paid. And the expenses of these gigs are horrendous. It seemed only fair that I have at hand a solid fee structure—in case things get out of hand.

My father-in-law, Daddybucks Wemple, under whose thumb I have labored with unsung selflessness for decades, pays me a pittance, but he slips his daughter Dorcas, my Tyranny Rex, enough extra to feed her cash-drain glass-blowing hobby featuring Tyranny's *piéce de résistance*—the urinating farm boy, to which she has recently added a new treat, the defecating cow.

I left the taxi at the corner of Imperial Highway and Pacific Coast Highway, a long block from the entrance to the airport grounds, and walked the rest of the way. These rich people have unlimited means to track you down and my privacy is my salvation. I have an unlisted phone, and the phone company answers it. My "office" telephone jack, without the phone, is between a false door and a wall. The door is always locked. It makes it seem like there was something important behind it.

Approaching the Imperial Airport Terminal I saw, through an array of chain link fences, the imposing silver jet parked on the tarmac with scattered secret-service look-alikes. It was adjacent to, but separate from, the hurly-burly of the big international sprawl next door.

The terminal building was simple, low and of the California Crate School of Architecture. It was the size and imposition of something you might find in a Mexican border town.

I was barely inside the gate when I was stopped by a secret service look-alike in a navy blue suit. Though the bombs that killed the other victims were sent in the mail, Harold Mattlock was taking no chances.

"How did you get here?" the guard asked, looking around for a vehicle that might be carrying a bomb.

"I took the bus," I said. He didn't believe me. But since I had the secret passwords, "Fantasy seven," I was escorted to the plane.

Up close, it looked like one of those twin-engine jets that might carry a couple hundred passengers commercially.

Upstairs, I was greeted by a comely young woman who seemed to hold the rank of flight attendant. She had that welcome-aboard way about her. The forward cabin was done up like a waiting room in an upscale plastic surgeon's office. Plush leather chairs in masculine brown were staggered on either side of an aisle. The carpet was thick and wall-to-wall. Low coffee tables with crystal cut-glass tops sat between the chairs—Mattlock's magazines, newspapers and books sat on them. I could imagine a lot of guys cooling

5

their toes here, waiting for the big gorgonzola. Not me. He came instantly to the forward cabin to greet me. He was a guy in his sixties, in shape, with a genial, but impassive, face that put me in mind of one of those dogs whose nose and cheeks seemed to be on the same geometric plane.

Harold Mattlock wore an oxford-brown business suit and a finely striped black and tan tie. I had never seen him photographed in a sport shirt; and I imagined, if he ever attended an employee picnic and played softball, he would do it in a suit.

If I saw Harold Mattlock coming down the street, I'd peg him for an old-fashioned history professor, and any number of other things before I would think "Billionaire."

He'd married a beautiful woman, half his age. He encouraged her in her chosen endeavor of writing books by buying several book publishing companies. They weren't terrible books, but they weren't very good either. They might have benefited from the editor's touch, but who would have the nerve? In exchange, she was there when he needed her for one social function after another, dressed to kill, and in his mind the prettiest of the lot. And he hadn't gotten where he was by being wrong.

In the back of the bus, Mattlock's private quarters were like that private room in a posh Beverly Hills boutique where the profligate went to view the extortionately-priced, *haute couture*. The entire width of the fuselage was employed as a sitting room. There were knockout fabrics on the chairs and a silken print of muted shades of silver and gold on the walls. The rear wall was all mirrors, and I was put in the difficult position of facing the mirrors. It was most distracting seeing myself every time I looked ahead.

Cordial was the word for Mattlock. He had become so successful by dint of hard work and a nose for numbers. His father had started him off by dropping dead suddenly and leaving him a newspaper in the outback somewhere. He sexed it up a bit, and goosed the circulation with scandals and big-buck contests, and he was on his way.

After the flight attendant brought us mixed nuts in a

silver dish and Evian in crystal goblets, Harold Mattlock got down to business. He was seated in the center of a love seat, his hands out to the side, giving him the outline of a pup tent.

"I never dreamed there could be anything this outrageous," he said. "Not until we started seeing the news reports that linked that bomber with this crazy conspiracy stuff. Seven of us! Rule the world! Imagine anything so stupid?" Mattlock's upper lip was curling. That seemed to be as emotional as he got. "I do know Gideon Golan, the Federal Reserve Board chairman, but the idea that Giddie and I would ever take it into our heads to rule the world is ludicrous. I know all the jokes about the president being less important than Chairman Golan, but don't believe it."

"Do you know any of the others?"

"Some, met others. I'm sure you realize we don't meet clandestinely and plan nefarious schemes for taking advantage of the citizenry."

He even *sounded* like a history professor.

"Did you know Winston Chambers, the CIA head?"

"Met him once or twice."

"Bob Fenster?"

"He was one of our advertisers."

"A big one?"

"Oh, yes. He's got quite a large company."

"United Motors, Philip Carlisle?"

"Also major advertisers. I have paid calls on both gentlemen to express my appreciation for their considerable business. We never spoke of ruling the world." He looked away. "Now they are gone." In a moment, he looked back at me as though he couldn't quite place me. "Let's see," he said, abstractly, "who else is there?"

"The mutual fund guy."

"Oh, yes. If I ever met him, I don't remember. I certainly don't 'know' him."

"They are large advertisers too, aren't they?"

"Yes, but I don't think what's-his-name?—the boss—bothers with that," Mattlock said. "At any rate, I didn't call on him like I did the others."

"Other than a conspiracy crank, can you think of anyone else who might have it in for the seven of you?"

He shook his head without thinking. "No one," he said.

"You have anything at all to go on?" I asked.

"The FBI does psychological profiles now on these birds, and I hear they are surprisingly accurate. They tell me he's twenty-five to thirty-five, white, unhappy childhood. Social loner, unmarried, or may have been briefly. Educated, may work in a job that doesn't challenge him." He threw up his hands, "Who knows?" he said, "half the people I know fit a lot of that description."

"Yeah, may save us from looking on an Indian reservation or at the YWCA."

He smiled, grimly.

"Is there anything else you seven have in common?"

He thought a moment. "Wealth," he said flatly, as though it were an unimportant fact of life.

"So, what would you like from me?" I asked.

"As I see it, we have two options," he said. "One is to find him and lock him up." He looked straight at me as though that chore was right up my garden path.

"What's the other?" I murmured—trying meekly to participate in the monologue.

"Convince him his theory is foolish."

"That might be a hard go."

"I know—I know," he said, shaking his head. "A man convinced against his will, is of the same opinion still."

"A-men," I said.

"I'm not a young man," he said, "but I'm not ready to pop off either. I should have fifteen or twenty good ones left in me, if I don't have to spend them looking over my shoulder." Now he looked me square in the eye again. "Can you give them to me?"

Wow, I thought. This dude has been fed some exaggerated tales about me, and he hasn't told me who did the feeding, so I inquired again.

"Depends," I said. "Who recommended me?"

He waved his hand as though that weren't important. "It was a young woman in Interpol who said you had helped them with an art con."

" Jane Eaton," I said.

"Yes," he said. "Is that good, or bad?"

"What?" I was daydreaming about her—"Oh, Jane—good...yes—*very* good. Jane Eaton was the Interpol moll in charge of art fraud in Zurich, where I wound up on my last assignment. Jane was very good to me—even after she put me in jail."

"Then you'll take the assignment?"

There it was—the inevitable question I couldn't escape. I paused as long as I thought I could get away with, checking myself in the mirror at the same time. "I have been thinking. You know you are asking a gargantuan task of a pretty small guy. Law agencies the world over are trying to catch this guy. No cigarillo so far. I'm not a miracle worker. It would be one costly endeavor, and right at the moment I am not flush with funds."

Mattlock cocked one eye like he was seriously fixing me in a gunsight just to give me the feeling he was all business. Not a lot of humor to him. I guess you couldn't get that rich if you thought things were funny.

"Mr. Yates, let's be frank. I am the sitting duck for not only this deranged bomber, but dozens of scam artists. I could spend ten million a day on people who claim they can protect me. I'm told you are different. You are known as a man who doesn't exude any macho airs, is most unthreatening, but has an uncanny knack for getting the job done. What's more, they say, 'He has the most persuasive, quiet confidence in himself which he backs up by working strictly on contingency. If he doesn't get the pigeon, there is no cigar.' Now *that* appeals to me, Mr. Yates. I am a man who can pay anything that is asked of me. But let me share with you a lesson I learned early on—ability to pay is no sign of willingness to pay. I didn't get where I am by simply paying at every opportunity. Those opportunities never end."

How to bring the conversation back to money without disappointing this zillionaire? This just didn't seem a case with a high probability for success. And I could spend way more than I ever had.

When in doubt, be humble.

"Mr. Mattlock," I said, and he didn't ask me to call him Harold, "I am flattered by your confidence. But I am not a rich man. My other cases have been within my means, but I don't see me having the funds to stick with something as big and crazy as this."

"So you want an advance—on expenses?"

I nodded.

"Would you dump tens of thousands on someone using an alias with no known address?"

"If I had your money," I said, "and someone was bent on blowing me up, I might let loose of a few thousand."

He seemed to relax. A few thousand was petty cash to him. He must have thought I was going to ask a million up front. "I'll bill you when I need to replenish the funds," I said. "Sort of revolving credit."

"Fair enough. Now, what about the fee if you are successful?"

"What's your life worth to you?" I asked, without putting on any macho airs.

After I left Harold Mattlock, I caught the bus that went between terminals, because no taxis graced this place. I knew I was being followed, so I lost myself in the main airport, zigzagged, then when I was sure I was clear, I got a cab to retrace my steps to Elbert Wemple Realtors, my day job, so to speak.

Daddybucks was frowning when he saw me. Any other expression would have been out of character. He *had* to express his dismay on sight of me. Dismay first, then find a reason for it.

The Wemple Real Estate warehouse had all the panache of a factory. Each person had a desk on the floor as though they were operating some machine that stamped out engine gaskets. Around the more important personages, or "Top Producers" as we refer to them in the real estate biz, were wood and glass enclosures which permitted Daddybucks to keep his eye on the top producers from the sternum up. Not only did he want to make sure no one was doping off, he also apparently liked to look at women's sternums.

I sat at his feet (at the foot of his riser that elevated him above the troops). He could see me anytime he wanted, the whole tamale, sternum and all. It was important to him to treat me like a mental deficient.

"Psst!" It was Daddy Wemple hailing me to his elevated presence. I took my time moseying up there, then helped myself to his cooled water. The water at troop level was room temperature. Daddybucks was saving money.

The vomit-brown suit Daddy Pimple wore to cover his naked blob was pretty well covered with dandruff. Los Angeles had their smog alerts, Elbert Wemple Realtors had their dandruff alert. We rated him light, medium, and heavy. The received wisdom around the shop was it was best to avoid Daddybucks on heavy days. My philosophy was always, simply: it was best to avoid Daddybucks every day.

"When's the last time we raised rents out in Gardena?"

I just looked at him. Was it a serious question? "About four years," I said.

"Raise 'em," he said.

"Okay," I said.

"Okay?" he said, as though I had given him a nonsensical response. I was still standing, you understand. I preferred to sit only when bidden. Sitting had a way of prolonging the visit. Standing, he could blink, and I'd be gone. But now I needed him.

"Okay," I said. "I'll work up the comps, show them to you, and we'll raise 'em."

"So why do you have to wait for me to ask you?"

"That superior judgment is what makes you the boss."

He eyed me suspiciously, as well he might. When I poured it on like that, a bloodhound couldn't smell any sincerity.

We stared at each other for a moment. Daddybucks scratched vigorously behind his ear. Heavy dandruff warnings were in order.

"I'll get right on it," I volunteered and tried to effect a fast exit.

"Just a minute," he said. Getting obeisance was tops on Daddybucks' list of priorities. I stopped in my tracks. "Why haven't we raised them?"

"Too many vacancies," I said. "Market doesn't warrant it."

"What about nuisance raises?" he said. "Five, ten bucks. Not worth moving over."

My big problem with this was I always wondered who needed the five bucks more, some tenant or Daddybucks, who still had his *first* five bucks and it was laying in some institution moldering or "compounding" as he called it.

"Market's been pretty soft," I opined. "People doubling up. Moving back to Mom and Dad. Lot of vacancies."

"Still?"

"Getting better," I said. "Let me test the market," I offered. "All the buildings—" be a nice project, I thought. Give me an excuse for being out of the office.

Tyranny Rex was my next hurdle. But when I got home, she was nowhere to be found. I went out back to commune with my cycads and palms. I had three triangle palms, the *Dypsis decaryi* and I planted them in, guess what? A triangle! But the different growth rates were strange. I had three different sizes, the largest about eight feet tall, the smallest two feet, but the way it looked they would all be the same size in a couple years. Nature is a great leveler. Will Durant, who studied civilization and filled eleven volumes telling his *Story of Civilization*, claimed that one of the lessons of history was that the gap between the rich and the poor must not get too wide—for when it does, the poor revolt. Apropos of leveling devices long ago in England, the poor went around killing everyone with smooth hands.

Now some guy was bombing people he thought were too rich and too powerful. Daddy Pimple made me understand the frustration.

There among my palms, many of which were growing to be as tall as I was, I formulated my plan. I had learned early in my "career" to be outrageous with the rich. Just as it was flattering to me to be thought capable of solving the crime of the century, so it was flattering to my rich clients to be thought capable of paying outrageous fees. Harold Mattlock had laid on me a very clever ploy about me having so much confidence I didn't even charge for expenses. If I had made the decision without thinking, I would have been licking his boots.

I went inside to use the telephone. There, surrounded by a menagerie of glass figurines, I placed the call.

Mattlock had given me his secret, private number and a new code word.

Harold Mattlock answered.

"Mortality prevention," I said.

"Nice of you to call." He really was a swell guy. I was so gratified to realize real rich guys didn't have to be like Michael Hadaad, my employer-nemesis in my prior two cases, or Elbert A. Wemple, realtor.

It was one of the reasons I was calling him back.

"Mr. Mattlock," I said. "I am intrigued by the case, but I'm not convinced I can begin to work the miracle you would like."

He listened patiently. Too patiently.

"A case of this elusive nature is going to be far-reaching and very expensive. I am afraid it does not lend itself either to my usual contingency arrangement, nor to me fronting expense money."

Still no sound from him. Had we been disconnected? I prodded him, "Shall I go on?"

"Certainly."

I made some adjustment in my larynx before I said, "Were this a case I was able to handle on a contingency, I would ask five million if I succeeded."

If he reacted, I didn't hear it.

"I am willing to scale that back to a million" (and I said it in a way that 'paltry' was implied) "with the following proviso:—You send me a modest petty cash fund of ten thousand dollars. As I spend five or more, I will bill you until I succeed in having the bomber arrested, or dead, or you decide you no longer wish my services. If this is satisfactory to you, I should like the million dollars in escrow with irrevocable instructions to release the money to me, under the aforementioned conditions. If during my employment the police or FBI or anyone else solves the crime, I would be

14

entitled to an honorarium of one hundred thousand dollars."

There was a dramatic lull in my monologue.
"Done," he said.

When I hung up the phone, I thought—it was too easy. He had expected to pay more. If a guy is worth billions of dollars, how much is his life worth to him? A million to him is the equivalent of ten dollars to me. Would I spend ten dollars to stay alive? Ask me after Tyranny Rex comes home.

And there was no horsing around with Mattlock; he had everything accomplished in under eight hours. The ten grand (I was prepared to settle for five) had been wired to my bank account, which I had legitimized with a d.b.a. Gil Yates, and the escrow agreement was faxed to my local fax shop while I was standing there. I verified it with the escrow company and called Mattlock to tell him I was ready to work.

"Good," he said.

I asked if he could arrange for me to meet with the other targets. While I waited for him to make those contacts, I read up at the library on all the conspiracy theories I could get my hands on. They had a nice array of magazines and newsletters put out by anyone who thought the Martians were out to get us or the CIA monitored all our movements.

My immediate goal was to learn enough about them so I could think like they did—to imagine what it would be like to believe that seven people ruled the world and to feel you had to kill them to save mankind.

People believe what they want to believe. And reading this hysteria, I tried to keep that in mind. I tried to picture this man reading this stuff and going, "Yeah, yeah. That's it!" without stopping to ask himself how these seven miracle men could bring it off without having the *National Enquirer* there with a photo crew. It reminded me of the satanic-ritual conspiracies where all these eyewitnesses swore they saw people eating babies, but no one could explain where the babies came from, or what happened to the bones.

I made a note of all the groups and meetings mentioned.

My next stop was a visit to my formidable wife, Tyranny Rex, and the pretzel box we call home.

Approaching Tyranny Rex was more and more predictable. She devoted her life to the design, production, sales and distribution of her glass figurines and every waking hour and rational thought was engaged therewith.

Time, too, has taught me that there are certain mysteries of life that it will never be in my power to fathom. Not the least of these is my wife's juvenile enthusiasm for her little glass mammals which depict the bitter end of the digestive process.

She was in the garage working on her "cow pies," as she put it. What sort of mind dreamed up that euphemism?

"Dorcas," I said. I didn't have a lot of trouble not calling her Tyranny to her face. What I had more trouble with was completing her name once I started it. The urge was to stop with Dork.

She may have answered with a low, barely audible, "Hmm?" And I may have just imagined it. She was hunched over the glass droppings and her torch, her face was covered with her welder's mask and she looked like a surfeited Martian. I don't know how I would be able to hear a "Hmm" in that situation, even if she shouted it. "HMM!"

"How's it goin'?" I shouted above the din, longing for the day when we still had room in the garage for a car.

Her mask made some motions I took to be positive.

"Have you been reading about this bomber business? The guy who thinks seven people rule the world—so he's blowing them up, one at a time?"

I know if the mask had been off she would have employed one of her handy deprecating remarks, but she just kept torching the pencil-thick glass until little patties plopped off the end, one at a time, not dissimilar to the actual function itself.

"Well, I'm kind of curious about it. I discovered there's a meeting tonight in Hermosa Beach—a group, I guess, talks about this stuff. I thought it would be a kick. Want to come?"

Plop. Plop. Plop.

A piece of pie.

3

I drove up Pacific Coast Highway to the address in the conspiracy newsletter, quaintly named *The Unlucky Seven*. "Public invited," it said. It was a large apartment complex and I thought the meeting must be in a recreation room. But the blurb said "Apartment 114."

There were four courtyards in the stucco complex, with two-story stucco cellblocks surrounding each.

The Hermosa Arms was pure stucco, unadulterated by half walls of brick, stone, wood or concrete block. The name appended to this stucco prison was a mixture of languages. Beautiful Arms. Though there was nothing here to remind me of arms, unless you made the leap from rifle and hand grenades to bunkers. And if anything was beautiful, I didn't see it. Apartment 114 was in the bottom quadrant in what seemed a most creative numbering system. The next quadrant over had the swimming pool and a few homo sapiens were gathered there sapping the last rays of a setting sun to make them gorgeous and to encourage skin cancer.

I had timed my entrance precisely at seven as the notice said that was when the festivities would begin.

The door to 114 was open. I knocked gently, then stepped inside to be faced with four of the faithful. Three fellas and a girl by my reckoning, though it could easily have been the other way around. I'd rather not say they gave me the creeps, but I can't at the moment think of anything more tactful.

Tonsorial and sartorial elegance did not seem *de rigueur* with the conspiracy crowd, and I suddenly felt over-dressed in my striped-madras sport shirt and fairly clean khakis. They looked like the kind of people you would want to cultivate if you had an interest in sadomasochism.

I introduced myself as Bill Shelly from Redondo, and I was given some first names in exchange. Won't have any trouble hiding here, I thought, everybody is hiding. I sat on the last chair, though no one asked me to, and the room plunged into silence. There was a bar with two stools that set off this living area, the size of a BMW—the small one—from the kitchen, the size of a pastrami sandwich—the large one. In the doorway, which must have led to the bedroom, hung dozens of strings of beads. We seemed to be waiting for someone else. Either that, or they were beginning the seance with a half hour of silent meditation.

Or maybe they were waiting for me to leave. I was considering it when a tall gangling guy with low-slung jeans and a nose ring parted the beads and made his entrance.

"Yo, Fritz," one of the faithful said.

Fritz made no comment. We were in the belly of the whale and Jonah was preoccupied making his self-conscious entrance through the esophagus. His beady eyes zeroed in on me and he gave tongue to what his cohorts hadn't.

"You fuzz?" he said.

My hand went automatically to my chin. "Why? Didn't I shave?"

This merited a snort from the troops.

"Cops," he hissed.

"Cops? Me? Hey, I saw an announcement. 'Open to the public,' it said."

"Yeah—public. Not cops."

I didn't like the way Fritz looked at me. The black eyes in his head seemed sunken beyond normalcy and gave me the queasy feeling they were lasers doing damage to my soul. He was not a guy, I thought, I would turn my back on.

"Hey, wait a minute. I read the thing. Sounded like you were asking for people. I'm interested in the topic, okay?

I work in real estate. I don't even know any cops."

The tall one seemed to relax. "What do you think?" He threw the question open to the floor just as another woman came in the front door. This one was more of a look-er than the sad sack on the couch between what looked like two bookends depicting Hell's Angels. Her lips were extra-ordinary. They looked like she was pouting and smiling at the same time. It drove me crazy. Her hair was straight, but loose, and tickled her shoulders. It was the color of pale Ginger Ale. Her designer body was clad in jeans (bottom) and loose-fitting, snow-white cashmere sweater (top). Our eyes met in a very friendly way.

"What do I think about what?" the newcomer asked the tall one back.

"This guy fuzz?" He pointed at me.

"*Him?*" she said. "You guys are nuts paranoid."

"Really, this is no big deal for me," I said. "You feel better if I go. I'll go." The tall one seemed to be considering a counteroffer when the new woman spoke up. "He leaves, I leave," she said magnanimously, and her intoxicating eyes locked on mine. Apparently they wanted her to stay, because we stayed—my heart was pounding as I stood up to give her my chair, but she waved me off and sank to the floor at my feet in one blur.

"All right, the meeting will come to order," the tall one said. "You don't know us," he said to me. "I'm Fritz. This here's my girl, Netta." My heart sank until he nodded at the punker hemmed in by the Angels (Hell's). He repeat-ed the others' first names, Buck, Dick, and Pinky and ended with, "On the floor there, your fan, that's Charlotte."

"The harlot," one of the sports chimed in. Charlotte didn't seem to notice.

"Keep out the personal stuff," said the squat one on the couch whose name was Buck. "So, Bill, what brings you out here?"

It took me a moment to tune in to the name Bill. Malvin and Gil I had pretty much mastered. The more names you took the more alert you had to be.

"Well, I was reading this stuff—about this bomber going after these guys he thinks are ruling the world and I just got interested."

Fritz, still standing, got a severe look on his face. "We don't condone violence," he said, "but we understand it. So what is it you want?"

I shrugged my shoulders. "I don't know, see what it's all about."

They finally began yammering in what seemed like couched language. It was the nature of conspiracy theorists to be suspicious.

As much as I understood what they were talking about, the gist seemed to be these seven powerful guys just ran everything, from electing presidents and congressmen to picking big judges, to controlling the economy. Their tentacles were in everything from banks to airlines; the media to the Internet. The info was ladled out with just enough condescension to keep me from getting uppity.

"Okay," I said, quietly, "but seven people? And the president isn't even one of them. Where do you get that? Why not fourteen people? Or a hundred?"

Fritz shrugged his burdened shoulders. "Just is, is all. And until they started blowing up, the big boys would kill to be next in the group. What do you think keeps a guy going after he's passed a billion or two? It's power. Nothing pumps up the ego like power. And there isn't anything that gives power like being one of The Seven."

"But who decides who gets in The Seven?"

"They do. Who else?" This came from my pal, Pinky, on the couch who seemed to me to be sitting closer to Fritz's insignificant other than the terrain warranted.

"Is the lineup of the real seven the same as the papers say?" I asked, sharing a poignant glance with Charlotte.

"Okay, you have your industries—your United Motors, and Softex," Fritz instructed me. "Just the biggest. No mystery there. Imagine the world without them can you?"

"Well," I mumbled, "Ford and IBM or something?"

That interruption didn't please Fritz. "The Federal Reserve Board chairman *controls* the economy. He's much more important to the way the world works than the president. Biggest money now is in mutual funds. The biggest fund is the Mayflower Fund—trillions of people's money under their tentacles. It's the secret government stuff you have to fear." Funny how when he got going, Fritz didn't sound like a hayseed after all. "The CIA isn't accountable to anybody. Imagine what they can get away with without leaving a trail. The media is everywhere. It is so inbred you don't know where one entity starts and another leaves off. Then that leaves our actions with other countries. The Foreign Relations Council has been the country's skull and bones for almost a hundred years. The man who heads it has untold power. Together they call all the shots: not only who is going to be president and what he does, but what we eat for breakfast."

All the troops seemed in agreement. It was "no sweat" imagining someone killing. The restrictions placed on their lives every day from gun control to where you could smoke a cigarette was frustrating enough to make you homicidal. "It builds," Buck said. "I can understand it."

Pinky added his small change, "If the head of the biggest tobacco company was on The Seven, we'd be smoking in airplanes, restaurants and any other damn place you want."

"Bet your ass!" said Dick, the other of Netta's bookends.

I felt Fritz's beady, laser eyes burn into my back as I left, only then realizing Charlotte had slipped out ahead of me.

On the way back to my car in the street, I fell in step with Charlotte. Could she actually have slowed her step so I would catch up?

"Have a good time?" she asked. The traffic on

Pacific Coast Highway was adding a whirring, grumbling background to our conversation.

"I guess, did you?"

"Oh, it's okay. I'm doing a book on conspiracy theories and these guys aren't the wackiest."

I was shocked to hear her talk like that to a stranger. Charlotte saw my reaction. "Don't worry," she said. "They're all still in there. Now the real meeting starts with a Martian as the guest speaker."

I laughed, nervously. Could I trust her? It looked like a rough crowd. I looked back to see if we were being followed, then I realized *she* could be doing the following.

"So how long have you been working on your book?"

"Eighteen years," she said.

"Oh—any thought of publishing it?"

"Someday, maybe."

"Another eighteen?"

"Maybe," she frowned.

"I'll bet you have a lot of material."

"Scads."

"Would you share it?"

She stopped walking and looked me in the eye. Her gorgeous face took my breath away. This was a ship that could launch the world's navies and still have gorgeous left over. "Why?" she asked. "You writing a book too?"

"No," I laughed to give her a sense of how ridiculous that would be. "But I find it fascinating."

"You're not a believer, are you?" she asked, her breathing on hold for my response. Trouble was I couldn't tell from the tone of her question what response she wanted.

"Don't really know enough about it," I said.

"You'll be in a better position to judge when you see my files," she said, and we moved on through the front gate of the Hermosa Arms to the sidewalk.

"Oh, great," I exclaimed. "When can I see them?"

She looked at me as though I were a guy who didn't get it. "Right now," she said.

"Wow—where do you live?"

"Not far," she said. "Want to follow me?"

"Sure. Where's your car?"

"Down here."

"I'll walk you to it."

"You don't have to. I'm not afraid."

"You should be," I said.

"Why?"

"Because, you are knockout gorgeous." Never in a million years would you find Malvin Stark speaking with such brazen, undisguised libido to a woman, but as Gil Yates, I surprised even myself with these bursts of unbidden concupiscence.

She looked at me and slowed her pace. She was looking to see if I was kidding. I wasn't. She realized it, and we walked on a few more steps until she stopped in front of one of those little red Mercedes-Benz convertibles. I forget what number they go by, but they retail off the shelf at around a hundred grand.

I had a good laugh. "Yeah, and my Rolls is just down the street."

"Good," she said, "follow me," and I'm zonked if she didn't get in the damn topless thing and start the engine. "I'll wait till I see the Rolls pull up," she said.

"Ah, yeah, ah, better keep on the lookout for a little Plymouth. I lent the butler the Rolls."

She smiled. Damn fine teeth.

On my way to my heap, I thought I felt a pair of laser eyes burning on me. I turned, but heard only a sudden rustling sound.

When I pulled the Fury up beside Charlotte, she said, "Follow me into the building. I have two parking spaces and my Plymouth is in the shop," and away she zoomed with me struggling to keep her in my sight. Then it occurred to me she might want to lose me, seeing my car and all. But at the next light, she ran a yellow and I had to wait. She pulled over until the light changed and I once again followed. This time to the Esplanade—the street of pretty high rises on the beach. She put her card in the slot to open the gate, waited until I got behind her, then we both drove in. Her two parking places were right next to the elevator. She didn't bother putting the top back up on her sporty toy. So I abdicated caution and left the Plymouth unlocked.

She punched the button for the elevator, then said, when we were inside, "Push Penthouse, will you?" If I hadn't seen the Benz, I'd have laughed again.

Instead, I pushed "Penthouse." Then Charlotte kissed me. Not too long, not too sexy, not simply friendly— just right. "I love to kiss in elevators," she said, "don't you?"

"Oh, yeah," I said, my eyes in a flat-out swoon.

"Ah, I'll bet you don't even have an elevator where you live."

I didn't argue. When the motion stopped in the box, she produced another card which she inserted in a slot to open the door.

The apartment wasn't so much a home as a Hollywood set for one of those sexploitation films. High-tech furniture and appointments, oil paintings of superb quality (*viz.* expensive) and bronze statues here and there: Giacometti, Matisse, Rodin.

"Don't tell me," I said, "you won the lottery."

"In a way I guess I did," she said, and dropped onto the white-leather couch and patted a cushion for me. I sank into the softest leather that felt like a baby's backside.

"Oh man," I said, running my hands over the couch. "Where did you get all this stuff?"

"My husband," she said.

"Oh oh," I said, jumping up. "And I'm in his parking space!"

She laughed and it came out like a Streisand song. "Sit down, silly," she said. "He doesn't live here."

"Where is he?" I asked, shaking.

"Probably wrapped around his bimbo," she said.

"Want to tell me about it?" I asked.

"If you sit down," she said.

I did.

"I married rich," she said, simply. "Plastic surgeon. I wasn't doing badly myself. Real estate. Top Producer. That's where I met him. He asked me if I'd go to bed with him if he bought this building from me."

"And you said 'yes'?"

"It was an eleven-plus million deal. And he kept his word. He even made an honest woman of me. For a while."

"How long were you married to him?"

"Long," she said. "Four years, seven months, and twelve days."

I looked out the picture windows on the full moon that seemed to be smiling at us. "What a sight!" I said.

"Every day is different—fog is low one day, clouds are high the next. It's exciting."

"So he just gave you all this stuff—or is it still his?"

"No, it's mine. I got a good settlement."

"Settlement? You mean you're divorced?"

"Of course, I'm divorced," she said. "What did you expect, he'd come popping out of the garbage disposal?"

"Only if you put him in there."

She laughed. "Hey, I was tempted more than once."

"But, geez, if he gave you all this, what does he have left?"

"Plenty, believe me. We both made big money. He'd build up the boobs and tuck the fannies of the rich and the wanna bes, and I'd sell them houses in P.V."

"Palos Verdes," I said, and almost slipped about my father-in-law living there. Instead I said, "I've been there."

"Whooper-do."

"Yeah," I said, "I'm well traveled." You could see the hump of the Palos Verdes Peninsula from her picture window.

She gave me another Streisand laugh.

"So how did you get interested in this conspiracy stuff?"

"I don't remember, it's so long ago. I was taking a Ph.D. Poly-Sci class and it seemed like a good ticket."

"But, you didn't write your thesis?"

"Nah, I was selling houses out here in the South Bay to make ends meet and right in the middle of my thesis I realized I had made more that year in commissions than I could make in ten years as a teacher, so I packed it all in."

"You still sell?"

She wrinkled her nose. "Only when I get real bored."

I wanted to ask if she slept with all her customers, but decided that would be ungracious. "So, what's your take on these conspiracies?" I asked.

"Mostly, it's crap. But you talk long enough, you're going to stumble on some truth whether you know it or not," she sighed. "But, mostly it's zombies and weirdos."

"So why do you keep going?"

"Hoping I'll meet Prince Charming, I guess," she laughed.

"Wouldn't you have more luck at night school?"

"Done that, too. And the answer is Prince Charming is scarce in all venues, but sometimes you stumble on him— or vice versa—at the strangest places. Like tonight." And this was Miss America talking.

I exhaled until I started tasting my lungs. "Tell me something, Charlotte—do these guys know how rich you are?"

"Maybe that's why they call me Charlotte the harlot. I'm Charlotte Wiggins by the way," she said, sticking out her hand for me to take. I did. Touching her in all facets was a delight. "My close friends call me Wiggy," she winked at me conspiratorially. "Why don't you?"

"Wiggy?" I said. "Really?"

"Yeah—for obvious reasons," she said. "And not only because Charlotte rhymes with harlot. I guess the boys at the conspiracy klatsch couldn't figure how else a woman could afford a car like mine."

"Oh, I'm Gil Yates by the way," I said. That seemed to amuse her. "So what kind of guy you think is blowing all these guys up?" I asked.

"Methodical for starters. Anybody can wait so long between blowups is some cool cookie. He knows his explosives."

"But, how can he keep it up? I mean is anybody going to be opening mail packages anymore?"

"Because he's clever," she said. "He'll get to them somehow. Well, he certainly is sending an explosive message," she snickered. "I'll bet he thinks he is frightening the conspirators so much they will give up ruling the world, and turn all those earth-shattering decisions like smoking on airplanes back to the peasants."

"Non-smokers, I hope."

"A-men," she said. Then she yawned. "Oh, excuse me—it must be getting late. Do you want to go to bed?"

Just like that. Miss America to Malvin Stark. Just like that.

4

I can't explain this attraction I have for the other gender. All I know is I don't have it as Malvin Stark. It's like I get a brand new set of pheromones when I become Gil Yates. Like I really was Clint Eastwood or somebody. I am not anxious to analyze it too closely, it might go away.

Wiggy was an expert on conspiracy kooks and, therefore, most valuable to my secret project. Of course, that wasn't something I could explain to Tyranny Rex, but at least it comforted me to realize I had a perfectly good excuse.

Before we tucked in her super-king-sized playpen, I knew I had to call Tyranny Rex. Before or after was the only question, but why do now what you can put off until later?

Later had arrived.

In her bed, I hoisted myself on my elbow to look at the most beautiful form I had ever imagined, and she was telling me what a lovely, gentle man I was.

"You really have the most perfect body," I said. "Like Venus de Milo with arms. Did your ex work on you, or is that the original version?"

She gave me a kiss on the cheek. "You're sweet," she said. "It's all me, unaltered."

"Whew," I fell back on my elbow, then propped back up. "Wiggy..." I said.

"You want to call your wife."

"I..."

"The phone's in the living room, another in the kitchen if you want privacy. Or you can use this one." She pointed to the sleek Danish thing on the nightstand.

I got up. "I better go to the living room. I don't want to bother you."

She was smiling as I left. The clock showed me a configuration of hands that seemed to indicate it was almost twenty after one. I started to punch the buttons on the phone that was neon lit, then abruptly hung up the phone, realizing I had no idea what to tell her. When I gathered my pitiful thoughts, I tried again. It was a groggy hoarse voice that said, "Hullo" on the first ring.

"Dorcas?" I wasn't sure.

"You idiot," she said. "Where are you?"

"I went to this thing like I told you. The conspiracy stuff in Hermosa. It's fascinating."

"I'm sure it is, but at this hour I'd rather not be fascinated. Did you forget I'm leaving for Chicago at six in the morning? You can't keep anything straight."

Of course, I *had* forgotten. "Well, I won't bother you," I said. "I'll stay over here, maybe with one of the guys. Have a great trip."

"I should be nice and rested," she said sarcastically, "having my sleep shot to hell in the middle of the night."

"Sorry," I said. "I'll see you when you come back."

"Where are you?" she asked, but I hung up the phone. Then I returned to paradise. Wiggy was still there. I don't know where I expected her to be, but I remember being pleasantly surprised.

After I had settled in beside her, I said, "Wiggy?"

"Hmm."

"May I see your files?"

She laughed. "See me, see my files. What a romantic thing to say."

"Yeah, I guess. Pretty dumb."

She tweaked my nose, then kissed my earlobe.

"You couldn't be dumb," she said. "You're too sweet. Of course, you can see my files—and anything else you want to see." She had the slyest twinkle in her eye.

"I'll never get tired of looking at you."

"You're sweet."

She looked out on the black ocean highlighted by the white rays of the moon. Then she turned to me kissed me with a sudden passion.

For some reason that elicited from me a physical response and our dialogue was *interruptus.*

The phone rang, startling me. My first, irrational, thought was Tyranny Rex was calling me. I almost reached for the phone, but Wiggy beat me to it.

"They hung up," she said.

"Who?" I asked.

"How would I know?" she asked with a touch of impatience.

"Your ex-husband ever pull that on you?"

She bestowed on me and my question a bitter chortle. "No," she said. "Could be a wrong number—too embarrassed to say anything."

"Umhum," I was not among the converted. "The bozos from the conspiracy coven have your number?"

"I don't know. I might have given it…" she trailed off in thought.

For some reason, I was not reassured.

"Probably somebody downstairs pushed the wrong button."

"You mean, your name is at the door?"

"It's a code. They can't tell which apartment I'm in."

I thought about that for a moment, groping for some reassurance. But I couldn't shake my uneasiness.

"So who do you think is blowing these guys up?" I asked, "A foreign terrorist?"

"I don't think so. They like to call attention to their causes. And they usually take credit. No, I think he's home grown. And that's nothing we should be proud of."

"Okay, but what's your gut feeling about conspiracies?"

She seemed to sink into the bed and become part of it. "Usually they don't exist. It may be disappointing that that runt Oswald shot Kennedy alone, but that's the size of it. The JFK conspiracy nuts have what they call the magic bullet theory that has a bullet going into Governor Connally every which way and coming out a direction that couldn't possibly have happened if Oswald was alone and above. But they draw Connally's figure as though he were facing front. But after the commotion he turned, so the path of the bullet, with him in that position, is perfectly logical. The guys who write these theories and who teach these courses—scoffing at the very idea a bullet could move so crazily—must *know* what really happened. It was written up in the Warren Report and they must have studied that—yet they continue to promulgate the fantasy that it's all a big cover-up."

"Say," I said as casually as I could, "what do you say we try to solve The-Seven thing? You and me, just for fun."

"Are you crazy?"

"No, no, just between us. And we could put a wager on it—see who gets to him first. Say fifty thousand dollars."

Her eyes shot open. "You can afford that much?"

"I expect I can," I said. "You?"

She nodded and looked at me with increased interest.

Wiggy and I agreed to keep in touch, sealing the bargain with a long and longing kiss. I spent the day at home trying to get organized. Someone said, "When in doubt, start at the top." So I called the FBI. I got right to the point. I had been hired to investigate privately, the mail bomber, and would appreciate any background information they could share with me.

I wouldn't say they laughed at me, nor could I make a strong case they didn't.

I called Harold Mattlock.

I waited only seconds for him to come on the line. "It's all set up," he said. "You can see the other three survivors. They'll make time for you. Just call them up." He gave me their numbers.

I told him what I had done and how the FBI had stonewalled me.

"You should have called me," he said. "I'll get you anything you want."

Practically, I was delighted to be granted that kind of access; philosophically, I was chagrined. Maybe there *is* such a thing as The Seven.

Mattlock called back in a matter of minutes. I could go anytime to FBI headquarters in Washington, D.C. or they would send a man to brief me.

"I'll go—pick up the Federal Reserve chairman at the same time," I said.

"Fly first class," he said.

I made a mild protest.

"I don't want you cramped up in coach breathing stale, short-rationed air," he insisted. "The airlines save money by pumping less air. More air, less people in first. Fly first. If I wasn't using my plane, I'd send it for you."

Mattlock supplied me with names and numbers of the victims' families, employees, and friends, and I got on the phone in my empty house. Everyone was cordial and wanted to help and were so sorry they were at a loss to make any sense of the tragedies. All that is except Bob Fenster's new wife, Jennifer. Mattlock had warned me she was still too distraught to speak to anyone, and her secretary confirmed it—gently, tactfully, and took my number in case Jennifer had a change of heart.

The calls only confirmed my premonition: This would not be an easy case.

I called the office and told the receptionist, "Tell Daddybucks I'm in the field all day working on comps for the rent raises."

"He's here," she said, "you can tell him yourself."

"No thanks," I said and hung up before that cornpone twang singed my ear. The delightful thing about the receptionist was she got the messages so garbled they weren't recognizable. But, she met Daddydandruff's prime criterion for hiring: she worked cheap.

If I remember Tyranny's schedule for Chicago—it was about five days. But I seldom remembered right. So I called another number.

Her voice was even more seductive on the telephone, and all she said was, "Hello."

"Are the files open?" I asked.

"*Every*thing is open," she said.

The sun's rays cut through to my bones and warmed the whole package.

I buzzed Wiggy from the street.

She "buzzed me in" as they say, and opened the elevator door for me when I arrived at her lofty penthouse. She was wearing the most becoming yellow sundress that fit just right. Her bronze legs held the whole thing aloft with the surreal perfection of a manikin.

She reached for me as if I might escape if she didn't hold me in place.

"I really came to see your files," I said.

She said nothing, her mouth pressing to mine in desperation. She seemed intent on testing my virility, maneuvering me to her bedroom in sort of a slow dance. There, I surprised even myself.

Exhausted, but happy, I propped my head off the pillow with the flat of my hand and I looked at her with one eye closed, the other half-opened. "You don't really have any files, do you?"

"Oh no," she said. "I have them."

"But you don't want me to see them?"

She nuzzled my neck like a squirrel hiding an acorn. "What's your hurry?"

Could it have been another hour before, naked in

her bed, I had the freedom and courage to bring up the files again?

"Tell the truth," I said. "You've been working eighteen years on a book and you don't even have any notes."

"That what you think?"

"Well, I've been here twice. I haven't seen anything that even looks like file cabinets."

She bobbed her nose left then right. It was a talent. Suddenly she leaped out of bed and startled me. "Follow me," she commanded.

"Hey—shouldn't we get dressed first?"

"No. Come on, or I'll cool off on showing you."

The next door down the hall was closed. Wiggy was standing in front of it, hiding none of her naked perfection, manipulating numbers on the knob to unlock it. On succeeding, she threw the door open, stood back and gestured with her arm thrown wide for me to behold the room.

I approached slowly, feeling like a heathen being invited into a secret religious inner sanctum.

Indeed there were file cabinets, lots of them. Three walls full. "Holy smog," I said. "This is all conspiracy stuff?"

She nodded, reluctantly, displaying serious second thoughts about sharing her personal secrets with a strange man who might ridicule her for having them.

"Remember our agreement," she said. "It's *my* book."

"How much of it have you written?" I asked.

"What?" She seemed not to have understood what I was talking about. "Oh," she said, "not much..."

"Eighteen years?" I said. "Surely you have at least a good outline and a bunch of chapters?"

She shook her head.

So that was it. Eighteen years yielded nothing but bulging files. If I came in and scavenged her files, then stole her book, the life would be drained out of her. She would be left with nothing but her incredible beauty. It was the pursuit of information that gave her life meaning.

"Well, there they are," she said, waving haphazardly

at the file cabinets on three walls. "My life's work. Maybe you'll make something out of it."

While I pondered Wiggy's mood as displayed in that last sentence (was it simply painful sarcasm?), she slipped out the door.

In less than a second, the bolt shot into place. It was certainly to my credit, that standing there naked, it didn't take me many more seconds to realize what had happened.

I tried the door. Locked solid. "Hey!" I yelled. Then louder. "HEY!"

There was no answer.

5

Telephone was my first thought—nine-one-one. There was a telephone jack, just no telephone instrument. Just like my "office."

I looked out the window. I could yell for help—but I couldn't get the window open. I was a little queasy about heights anyway and I don't know what an open window twelve or so stories up would do for my nervous system.

It had to be a joke, I thought. Then I heard the front door open and close and there was silence after that.

"Wiggy?" I called out. "Charlotte?" Nothing. Did I learn my lesson about beauty being as thick as the skin? Getting intimately involved with a stranger? Could *she* be the bomber? That's crazy, I thought. But on second thought, no crazier than locking me naked in this room.

Was it a sudden inspiration, or had she planned it?

Maybe the answer was in the files. I reached for the nearest drawer, thinking it would be locked.

It wasn't. It was a momentary high. I ran naked around the room pulling open file drawers. *They all opened*! And they were all stuffed with folders. I started pulling them out and leafing through them quickly to get a feel for what she had. She had *stuff*!

For the next untold hours, I pored over Wiggy's research. She was meticulous.

Drawer upon drawer crammed full of folders with enticing labels:

Psychological profiles of serial killers

Conspiracy theories:

with subheadings:

JFK

ABRAHAM LINCOLN

VINCENT FOSTER

CIA

AIDS

HITLER,

and on for miles.

I decided it was better to be locked in the room than locked out of it. But I was so knocked over with the copious information in the files, I stopped thinking about how I was going to get out of my prison.

Until I saw the sun beginning to sink over the edge of the ocean. Then, I started to get hungry. My next thought was Wiggy was going to starve me to death. Maybe she had an Edgar Allan Poe fetish.

My emergency plan was to break the window and yell for help. The trouble was the apartment was so high you couldn't see the people walking and biking by on the strand below. So, I would have to attract the attention of a swimmer who had waves crashing all around him. I looked out, but didn't see anybody in the ocean. It was too late.

I turned morose at the thought of never being able to leave my cell—shriveling up, dehydrating to a pile of bones in the penthouse on the Pacific. True, I would be a pile of bones with a warehouse of knowledge on conspiracies, but a useless pile of bones nonetheless.

Despair brought me down. I took a break from reading Wiggy's research and devoted my attention to self-pity. Finally at my nadir, I picked up the chair I had been sitting in and threw it at the window.

It bounced off the glass and hobbled back across the floor.

Naturally. Tempered glass.

Suddenly I noticed the air conditioning seemed to come on full blast and I shivered in my skin trying vainly to find a corner of the room where I might keep warm.

Then I looked for something to cover my body—a blanket, a rug, anything I could pry loose. But the room was a workroom. The chair at the computer had a cushion attached to the seat. There were no blankets, rugs, pillows. I could just see myself dying of double pneumonia.

I looked for the vent and saw it in the top of the wall. I rolled the chair over to it, then stood precariously on the chair and tried to close the vent, but whether painted open, rusted, or bent, I couldn't budge it. I was getting angry when I was stunned to hear the phone ring once. It was the signal someone was at the door. In a minute, it rang again. If only I could answer! If only I could communicate, I'd let in Jack the Ripper in my predicament. Was this, I wondered, the same guy who rang when I was closeted with Wiggy in her bedchamber? Fritz or one of his savages?

I was lying on the floor, resting, but my heart was pounding as if I had finished first in a triathlon. My mind raced with absurdities. Like, maybe, Wiggy was the killer. It would make sense that she had all this material on serial killers if she was one herself. It didn't dissuade me that women didn't fit the profile of these nuts. I reasoned she had proven with her sex drive she had a passel of male hormones. I was lying there breathing like a locomotive and storing up energy for a last-ditch attempt to save myself like Superman when I heard the front door open. My first thought was Wiggy had sent an ape to tear me from limb to esophagus. But the footsteps seemed light. Maybe it was Wiggy with a gun. To make it look like she shot a naked intruder?

There was a gentle knock at my door. I didn't respond.

"Gil, you still in there?" she asked, and her voice sounded different.

"Where did you think I'd be?"

"Finding everything all right?"

"Wiggy—open the door, please."

There was a long silence.

"Please," I pleaded. "I'm hungry."

Another quiet time. "Oh, all right," she said. "I only locked it for your own good."

"Some good."

And the door opened, but Wiggy didn't come into the room. It was as though she felt she might be contaminated if she crossed that threshold. She was dressed in a lime shirt-dress and looked casually disheveled, but still good. Then the alcohol vapors hit me.

"Wiggy—have you been drinking?"

She scratched her nose. "I may have had a glass of wine," she said.

"What about food?" I asked. "You have any food in the house?"

"Come on," she said, then she tittered. "Why, you don't have any clothes on! I guess you should get dressed— or I should get undressed. What do you think?"

"Food," I said, hoarsely. I never thought I'd ask for food first, but it gave me an insight into our innate priorities.

"Well, come on then," she said, turning her back to me, "I brought Chinese."

And if she hadn't dished it out to us both from the same paper containers, I'd have suspected she might be trying to poison me, until I began eating. I was so hungry it didn't seem to matter.

I had put on my pants and shirt and was gobbling down a mishmash of veggies and exotic sauces when I noticed Wiggy was only playing with hers.

"So why did you lock me in there, Wiggy?"

"Oh, I don't know," she said. "Maybe, I couldn't bear the files coming between us. It's like a separation anxiety. I mean, I have eighteen years wrapped up in there and you come along to steal the fruits of my labor."

"Why would I steal it? You're letting me copy it."

"I don't care. Write the book, do what you want. I'm a collector with no follow-through. A pack rat of notes and material. I don't ever want it to end. And it never does end. One conspiracy theory spawns another. I can go on forever without ever writing my book. I was going to call it *The Conspiracy of Conspiracies*—like it?"

"I love it."

"You can have it."

"I don't want—"

"Yes, yes. Take the title too. Bury my name on the acknowledgment page, somewhere below your wife and children. I don't care."

"Wiggy—I'm not in this to write a book."

"It's okay," she said, sniffling, "you don't have to deny it."

She was so pathetic, I wanted to tell her the truth. But I couldn't. After all I *had* harbored notions she was the killer. When you are cooped up naked in a locked room you have time to harbor notions.

"Now, do you want to go back in there or shall we go to bed?"

I *was* pretty tired.

6

The FBI building in Washington, D.C. was a gloomy place—the stark facade, the concrete walkway to the entrance, unbroken by any art or tree. Even the handful of people sitting on the bench awaiting the next tour of the premises seemed gloomy.

It was a stark contrast to the penthouse on the Pacific I had just left and my sunny hostess, Wiggy. She had wanted to come along to Washington, but I had put her off with a promise of calling for her when I got a grip on where to look for our bomber.

She had sent me off with remarkable reams of computer printouts with Eastern Seaboard conspiracy bugs and groups. Sifting through them could take a lifetime. But I missed her already as I compared her *joie de vivre* to every downer I met at the FBI.

Inside the building, a young black woman, fluorescently lit, and gloomy, asked if she could help me. I said, "No thanks, I'm beyond it," but she didn't smile. She wore a telephone headset that pressed her ear on one side of her head, her temple on the other, in such a way it seemed to make smiling out of the question.

"Actually," I said, "I'm here to see Agent Fan."

"First name?" she said.

"Mine or his?"

"His."

"Mark, I think."

She fiddle-faddled with a computer keyboard, her hard eyes fixed on the console screen. It looked from her expression as if there were a ton of Fans, and they were all on her back. But finally, she poked a keypad and as if shouldering a black woman's burden, she waited for a response. From the attitude she radiated, you'd think I had asked her to lift a taxicab.

She seemed surprised when she told me Agent Fan would see me. Of course, I had to wait until authorized personnel came to guide me through the top-secret labyrinth. No kidding, that's what she said, "Authorized personnel."

So I waited. I had arrived the night before and checked into my room at the Hay-Adams Hotel, overlooking the White House lawn. Mattlock had arranged for the hotel, too. "No Holiday Inns when you are working for me," he had said.

After Harold Mattlock insisted I fly first class, I posed myself a question. Would flying in that relative luxury lessen my fear of flying? And, I think it might have. At least I felt if I went out in a crash, I would be doing it in style. Albeit under a phony name.

"Mark Fan," a voice said, in front of me while I was reliving my first-class experience.

I looked up and there was a guy in solid middle age that I suppose had some Chinese in his ancestry, though it looked suspiciously as if some gringos had polluted his blood. Here he was, 'authorized personnel' personified.

We shook hands. He had a very nice grip. He asked for some identification, and I showed him the best Gil Yates stuff I had—a license gotten up by a friend of a friend.

"Follow me, please," he said, and I did, through endless corridors and enough stairways to burn off my lunch. Agent Fan, I decided, was a fitness freak. Either that or he was trying to wear me out. Or confuse me so I couldn't retrace my steps.

At last, we arrived at a windowless room (gloomy) and he waved me to one of the two chairs therein. Windows, I decided, were a breach of security. Outsiders could not only climb in them, but they might also photograph documents through them, even though they would need a helicopter at most levels to accomplish that.

"You must know some big people," he said, as he took one metal chair and I took the other in his spartan office.

"Oh?"

He had a curt nod and he used it. "We don't ordinarily dance for outsiders here. Not on something this big." He did not seem a happy dancer.

"Maybe I'm a big person."

He looked my face over, gravely, like I was a cadaver he was trying to place. He shook his head. "Big," he said. "So big I'd recognize you. Anyone would."

"That big?" I said, but I didn't commit.

"So, what can I do for you?"

I told him.

He nodded. "That's what I'm told," he said. He opened the middle drawer in his desk and pulled out a folder, my guess was four-inches thick. It could have been more.

"Here's what I've culled for you. We have a hundred times this, maybe two hundred. Look it over. Need any more help, call me." I got the impression Agent Fan would not have been unhappy if I thanked him and left. Maybe he could have lived without the thanks.

"Do you have any idea where the guy lives? I mean, what part of the country?"

"Explosion obliterated postmark on two. One was traced to Seattle. But we think he travels and mails from different parts of the country. We don't have a good fix on where he's from. Fairly big city be a good guess, but we have no evidence. We've done psychological profiles and, on the one hand, we come up with a big-city loner, probably Eastern, but when we diddle with the dials a little, they produce a mountain man from the wilds of Wyoming or Montana—maybe Alaska. So, what I have to tell you is, we don't know."

"What are you working on?"

"Finding him."

"How?"

"Any lead is followed up. We interview all these guys who are known to swallow The Seven theory."

"Any luck?"

"When you consider the theory on its face, you don't expect much cooperation with law enforcement. Certainly not the FBI. Maybe you'll have better luck; you're not connected to an institution. Might be less threatening to them."

"What about tips from the public?"

He nodded. "We get lots of them."

"Check them out?"

"We don't overlook anything with the least legitimacy."

"What percentage would you say are legitimate?"

"Depends. Maybe one in fifty has some substance—and we'll check, maybe five in fifty. If there's a reward offered, it's more like one in two hundred."

"Any suggestions?"

"If we knew, it has already been tried and failed. There is no magic secret to these things. Be a lot easier if there was. Persevere. It's dog work, you just keep at it. They say it's dumb luck sometimes that nails the bird. If that's true, it's dumb luck that follows eons of scut work." He threw out his hands. "What else can I tell you?" He wasn't really asking me the question as much as commenting on the hopelessness of it.

"You take some pleasure from your work?" I asked him. It didn't look like he did.

"Oh, yeah," he answered. "'Course, there's a lot of frustration, lot of dead-ends. But you get used to it. When you hit something there's a lot of satisfaction, yeah. You?"

I hadn't expected the tables to be revolved. "I'm in it mostly for the money," I said. "But, sure, anytime you knock yourself out over something and it works, there's satisfaction."

Then I noticed for the first time, there was nothing

on Agent Fan's desk but the folder. It was perfectly clear, not a picture, a pencil, paper, nothing. More security?

I changed the subject. "What about his method?"

"What about it?"

"Can he keep it up? Nobody is opening their own mail anymore."

He nodded. "Man knows his targets. Very thorough. One was from a girlfriend—marked 'PERSONAL' with her return address. Guy thought he was on the receiving end of an unexpected gift. Couldn't let anyone else open it."

"How do you know that?"

"Secretary told us. She saw it first. She knew. She was in the next room when he blew up. Bang! Right on target."

"That was before he came out with the 'Seven' word."

"Yes, it was."

"How did that get out? Are you sure it was from the same bomber?"

"We aren't sure of anything. It could be different bombers, could have been the secretary, but we doubt it. We aren't as sure that the bomber leaked his goals. Could have been someone else—but it does seem to fit. We are familiar with The Seven theory. It's not new."

"Did you have a suspicion before he leaked it?"

"Soon as the first one was hit," he said, "we speculated. Get a bomb in the mail, that's federal. They're messing with the big boys."

"Deliberate?"

"We think so. Adds to the challenge. They go against cops in Podunk, they aren't doing very much. They go against the bureau, they know they got a real opponent."

He was proud of his outfit. I just wondered if he knew how gloomy they all seemed.

"You have a psychological profile on the guy?"

"Sure," he said, pointing to the folder of stuff. "In there."

"Who made it up?"

"We have a bunch of shrinks around here. Always

trying to psych out the perpetrators."

"Think I could talk to one of them?"

"I don't see why not. You're talking to me, aren't you? Any guy with your connections can have the run of the place. But why don't you read her report first. She probably can't add much to that."

I could see he'd had enough of me. I stood and thanked him. He was on his feet in a flash.

"I'll show you out," he said, and he did. Just as silently as he brought me in. Had he been any faster, I wouldn't have had time to pick up my folder.

I had over two hours before my meeting with Gideon Golan, the chairman of the Federal Reserve Board, so I walked back to the Hay-Adams where there was much gracious bowing and scraping in the lobby. I bowed back (without the scraping) and went to my room to study the FBI dossier.

All that obeisance must have been what Daddybucks Wemple enjoyed when he went anywhere.

7

The desk in my hotel room looked like something the Johns, Hay or Adams, might have used, but not very hard.

The room itself was cozy, on an upper floor, and was decorated in something that might be referred to as Third Empire by someone who knew what that meant. To me, it just meant the stuff looked old; like it had been sitting in the hotel since John Adams was president. And very few people had touched it since. Sort of new old. Musty pink-beiges, but class.

I spread the FBI file out on the fancy desk and tried to make sense of the wealth of material.

The psychological profile caught my eye first. Boilerplate disclaimers started the piece. In essence, it said the profile was only speculation about possibilities. These were the "probabilities":

A white male between the ages of twenty-five and thirty-five. An unhappy or unsettling childhood—possibly abused by those who had power over him: parent, stepparent, teacher. A man at odds with his time and environment, a social loner. Probably his first murders. Employed in a city—New York,

Philadelphia, Washington, D.C., Boston, San Francisco, or Los Angeles most likely. Texas another possibility.

A college graduate, perhaps, not working to his full potential. A man with promise not fulfilled. Lives alone, and we cannot rule out a mountain existence in one of the mountain states—the means of livelihood in that circumstance being more problematic.

I didn't find anything in that profile I couldn't have written myself after reading the first newspaper article. It was pretty much what Mattlock had told me. It did narrow the population somewhat, but even if it was right on the dollar, we'd probably be left with around ten million guys to choose from.

There was a diagram on how the bombs were made, and it was frighteningly simple. A second diagram showed how a slightly altered bomb could fit into a plain number-ten envelope.

I got to the thick pile of papers that held the names of known people who at one time or another harbored some belief in The Seven conspiracy—or the nine—or any variation on a theory that certain people or positions in society were so powerful, the rest of us were pawns.

I wanted to compare the names on the FBI list to the names on Wiggy's list, but I didn't have enough time. I would do that when I returned from seeing the Federal Reserve Board chairman.

I took the FBI folder to the front desk and asked them to put it in the safe. They gave me an understated claim check, and I had visions of my folder reposing in the safe with a collection of state secrets from all over the world.

I ventured out and walked virtually next door to the

Federal Reserve Building. The bankers and their employees were more cordial than the FBI. The building was less gloomy and so was the help. Who said money was the root of all evil?

I was ushered, with a smile, into the office of Chairman Golan. It was an impressive office in size and third-bureaucracy decor. My guess was it was the equivalent of six or eight Agent Fan's offices, but this was where the money was.

The chairman stood and took my hand and greeted me like I was a celebrity honoring him with my presence. "Nice of you to come," he said. "Sit down, please. May we get you something?"

"Oh, no thanks."

His countenance was neither lovely nor ordinary. It looked as though someone had taken his face apart, piece by piece and then when trying to reassemble it, forgot how it all fit together. The nose was still in the middle all right, and the eyes, mouth and ears were in the right vicinity; they just didn't look like they fit.

But he was a very nice man—and brilliant, and not aloof. I couldn't see him as a man with any aspirations to rule the world or to take the slightest advantage over his fellows.

After a minimum of friendly little-talk, I asked if he could put himself in the bomber's skin. "Can you get a fix on why he's after you?"

"Do I know how he thinks?" he said. "I don't think he thinks very clearly. I think his actions are more emotional than rational. Seven people rule the world? How could a deep thinking intellectual come to that conclusion? Even once he's settled on a theory that four, five billion people are being manipulated in all their actions, all at the behest and for the benefit of these puppeteers, how does he settle on the number seven? Bible has some mystical sevens—a lucky number? Notice the pope isn't in there—or the president of the United States." He shook his head dolefully.

"I'm on a salary—as was the director of the CIA.

What are our chances of being enriched?"

"He thinks, I believe, it's just a lust for raw power."

He smiled. "Yeah. Me? Some power. First of all, I am the chairman of the Federal Reserve Board, not the whole board. We are a committee. We vote—majority rules. I don't tell them how to vote. How long do you think they'd stick around? These are men preeminent in their field. They have better things to do than rubber-stamp my decisions."

I nodded. "Yeah, well," I said, "why do you think he's after you?"

"I don't know. Fantasy."

"If you *had* to ascribe a reason to his actions—relative to you—say he was a cut above a blithering idiot and had some reasoning powers—why would he *think* you were so powerful?"

He sat back in his chair. He folded his hands on his lap. "You know, don't think I haven't thought about it. And don't think I'm blasé about it. The chairman of the Federal Reserve Board is not one who should have to expect assassination. The president—it goes with the territory unfortunately—but there never has been a Federal Reserve chairman even shot at. It's bizarre. If we want to flatter ourselves, we might think our actions have some effect on the economy. Others might say we only react to the economy, and our reactions have negligible effect. Too late, some say. The economy is so vast and so complex no one person or seven or five hundred are going to control it. We push up or down the discount rate we charge banks to borrow. A quarter percent, a half percent—the banks adjust their prime rate. So what? That rate has lost all its meaning. It used to be for the big guns only—United Motors could borrow at prime, you and I would pay more. Now Joe Blow can borrow at less than prime. And the banks don't all fall in line with us. Often we'll lower rates and they won't. We can't compel them."

"You think this bomber doesn't know that?"

He shook his head and sighed. "Sorry, I'm rambling.

Nerves, I guess. Here's his only link that I can see. And I really don't peg him as this intelligent. Frank Smithson is on the list—The Seven—head of the Mayflower Mutual Fund—the biggest—like a couple trillion in assets. We—the Fed—control the amount of money that is released into the economy by the government."

"You mean, you just print money?"

"Essentially, yes—but not an infinite amount. It is carefully controlled so it won't upset the applecart."

"What's the applecart?"

"Inflation, I'm talking about. Anything we release into the economy is inflationary per se."

"But we haven't had much inflation lately."

"Exactly!" he exclaimed. "Further proof that nobody can predict the results of our actions, let alone manipulate them. There used to be a direct correlation between the 'M' factor—the money released into the economy and the rate of inflation. But some years ago, a curious change took place. Inflation seemed to be absorbed and offset by the stock market. And the stock market today is largely driven by mutual funds. The money we used to release went for goods—a new TV, a car; and services—a fast-food meal, doctor's fees. And that was inflationary. Pushed up the costs—created more demand. Now that money has been channeled into mutual funds—savings—and the stock market has inflated, some say beyond reason."

"What do you say?"

"I don't buy stocks," he said. It was a partial answer.

"So that's how this murderer ties you in with The Seven, you think?"

"It's all I can imagine. Money we release goes to mutual funds. But there are thousands of them now. Sure Smithson's Mayflower is the largest. Theoretically he benefits the most. So every time the board releases money, he gets part of it. But in the scheme of things, what he gets, as the result of my actions, is ludicrous."

"Do you know him?"

"Smithson? Yes."

"Can you quantify how much money Frank Smithson could make personally in a year from the money you release into the economy?"

"I couldn't begin to guess. I don't know his setup. But his wealth is staggering. Whatever is added to it because of some action of the Federal Reserve Board is so negligible. He already has more money than he could spend in a hundred lifetimes if he were a drunken sailor. When you think about it, nothing gels."

"But does it add to his *power*? His prestige?"

He waved the question away with his hand. "At most, it adds to his wealth and power relative to the wealth and power of all these other mutual funds. If he has three-point-two percent more than the next guy, that probably won't change."

"How about the opposite? If you don't release money, what happens to the mutual funds, and the economy?"

"Funds would probably level off. Not a bad thing in my judgment. Economy could stagnate, not a good thing in my judgment."

"Have you been contacted personally by this bomber?"

"No."

"Any notes, subtle threats, through others? Anything mysterious at all?"

"Nothing that hasn't been in the news and nothing personal."

"Do you think your name on the list could be a mistake?"

He sighed. His head moved to the left and back again. It was a half a "No."
"Anything is possible, I guess," he said, brooding. "I only wish I believed it."

"Are you frightened?" I asked him.

He looked at me like he thought I should be in a cage somewhere. "Of course, I'm frightened. Scared to death. I don't go anywhere. I don't touch mail. I look over my shoulder when I walk to my car. Every noise I hear at night sets my heart racing. I still have a lot to live for. My children are starting families. I have two little grandchildren already. I'd like to see them grow up."

"Have you thought of resigning?"

"Of course, I have."

"Are you going to?"

"I haven't ruled it out. It's so...so cowardly though. It's like I want someone else to be the target. How easy would it be to fill the job? Would you take it?"

I laughed. "Would you offer it?"

"If I did—assuming you were qualified?"

"Probably not. If there were any heroic genes in the family pool, they passed me by."

"So you see," he said and spread his hands in a hopeless gesture.

"Well, maybe they could dissolve the board, temporarily, or reconstitute it."

"Give in to a murderer? We don't capitulate like that in this country," he said, but I was not convinced he would personally oppose capitulation. "Well, if you are finished," he said, "I'll get back to work."

I couldn't think of anything else to ask, so I shook his hand, thanked him, and asked him if he would be good enough to call if anything unusual happened that might help my investigation. I gave him the number. He told me to call him any time. Then he fixed me with a most desperate pair of oddly placed eyes, like he was watching his life slip away.

"Find him," he pleaded.

8

I was missing Wiggy and her extra-soft touch. So, I called her on the thinnest pretense, half joking, that I needed her help. She told me she would be on the next plane, and before I could protest, she was.

I wished I had been able to shake my suspicion about Wiggy. Too many women who are eager lovers turn out to have an agenda of their own. Not only was Wiggy an amorous delight, she was curiously eager to join me in my pursuit of the killer. But what if I were pursuing her...?

On the one hand, it seemed impossible that she was the killer. She was so sweet and loving...and *beautiful*! On the other hand, she was a bit kooky—wiggy even. I didn't want to believe she was capable of such a thing, but neither did I want to make some foolish blunder that might get me deep-sexed. Sex is six in German, isn't it?

I decided the thing to do was keep Wiggy close by so I could keep my eye on her. See how she reacts to things I do and say. Try some ideas on her. See if she is too quick to endorse ideas that would leave her out, too eager to pooh-pooh scenarios that might fit her.

I had no shortage of speculations, having had the relative luxury of thinking time with Wiggy at the other end of the country. That was another reason it was a mixed blessing having her join me. I was actually looking forward to trying some of my ideas out on her. Like the Tylenol syndrome.

While Wiggy was in the air, I paid a call on Dr. Hazel

Vaughn at the FBI. Dr. Vaughn was in the throes of some nasal catastrophe which must have caused a significant jump in the stock of the makers of the tissue she was saturating with her abundant sinus fluids.

She would stake her reputation that one man did all three bombings, she said, but she was less sure of everything else. "The psychological profile is probably as close to the money as you can get," she said between blows, "but the rest is conjecture at this point." I left her as soon as I could. I didn't want to catch what she had and I was sure those microbes were making their way through the secure air-circulation system in that gloomy building. I was as vulnerable as a transcontinental airline tourist passenger.

The Washington, D.C. airport was in Virginia, but it might as well have been in Texas. You could figure your travel time in two halves: the first, the flight; the second, getting to town from the airport.

At airports I usually park at the curb until a cop chases me. Then I drive around the airport to save the parking fee until the visiting party shows up on the curb.

I made an exception when I met Charlotte Wiggins. I parked the car and went to the gate to meet her. I was on an expense account.

She came bounding off the plane looking radiant as ever, with a gait that put you in mind of someone effortlessly riding a pogo stick on a cloud. Her short, full skirt flounced as she did.

Her two tanned legs (but not too tanned) poked effortlessly out of her pale blue short skirt. They looked as if they had been turned on a lathe by a superior craftsman. And it was hardwood, oak or teak; there was no jiggle in them when she walked.

We embraced like lovers and I felt what I'd expected under the knobby, gray sweater. "No bra?" I whispered.

"Don't worry," she said, "it's just for you."

And everyone on the plane, I thought.

Wiggy's luggage reminded me of her Mercedes. Top of the line with some designer's initials plastered all over it.

That was another advantage of not meeting the plane inside the terminal: you didn't have to schlepp suitcases. And did Charlotte Wiggins *have* them! About four hundred before I lost count.

"Well," she said when I commented—"you didn't tell me how long I'd be here. It could be a few days."

"You know there is so much ground to cover," I said. "I really appreciate your coming."

"I missed you," she said. "I haven't had anyone to lock in the room."

"Oh, you do that to everybody?"

"No, only those I want to keep."

After we stashed the bags in the room at the Hay-Adams and Wiggy ducked into the bathroom, I decided on a quick check-in with the receptionist at Elbert A. Wemple and Associates, Realtors.

Darn if she didn't trick me. As soon as she said, "Elbert Wemple Realtors," I said, "Darlene," and she said, "One moment please," as though she didn't know who I was. She put me on hold and the next voice I heard was none other than that insufferable bore, Daddybucks Wemple. And the big, bad wolf was blowing steam like a ruptured hot-water pipe in the girls' locker room.

"Malvin you turd, don't you hang up on me now, if you know what's good for you. I'm hopping mad, Malvin. Where the hell are you anyway? All hell is busting loose in Long Beach and I've got an absentee supervisor. You want to keep your job, Malvin? Any desire at all to stay gainfully employed? Pay the mortgage—put food on my daughter's table—keep body and soul together in that little love nest of yours? Huh? Answer me, Malvin—you didn't hang up?"

"I'm thinking."

"Yeah, well think hard Malvin. We need you around here like another hole in the head. You want to play hooky for permanent, just let me know. Darlene, the receptionist, is itching for a promotion."

"Yeah, give her one. Wouldn't be my job. That would be a step down salarywise."

"Damnit, Malvin, you know damn well I'm paying you more than you are worth. Always have. So do you want the job or not?"

"I'll give your offer some thought."

"What offer?"

"Your golden parachute. Isn't that what they call them? I've been in harness what, now, twenty-five years? Maybe it's time for the gold watch and the huge retirement bonus."

"Are you crazy?"

"What with the kids pretty much gone and Dorcas doing so well with her diuretic cow, maybe it's time for me to putz the palms full time."

"Malvin, you're nuttier'n a fruit cake. How the hell would you expect to live on what Dorcas makes?" Then he paused to consider his own words. "Why, hell, she doesn't make anything, does she? All I do is write checks to prop up that madness."

"Well, I'll be thinking. Maybe I could go into the palm and cycad business."

"Sure, and some multimillionaire will just drop a couple hundred grand on you."

Billionaire, I thought.

"Are you there, Malvin?"

"I think I need some time off," I said. "Travel a little. See our son."

"The ballet dancer?"

"Yeah." I knew that would rile old Daddybucks—it never failed—and it delighted me.

"Damn sissy profession."

"More than real estate?" I needled him.

"Damn straight," he boomed, "only fairies dance on their toes."

I've seen some realtors do some fancy footwork, but I didn't say so.

"That kid is an embarrassment to us all," he said.

"Not to me," I murmured. I did love my kids after all, even though they seemed to stretch the basis for that from time to time.

"Well, hell," he groaned, "you never *did* have any judgment."

"Yeah," I agreed meekly, "maybe that's why I need the time off."

"How much time you thinking?" he grumped.

"Couple months should do it."

"Couple *months!*" he exploded. "Hell's bells, you think this is some kind of playschool?"

"No—I was just thinking how you always said the secretary could do my job on her lunch break. Now'd be a good time to test it out."

"Yeah, well, she's got her hands full answering the phone."

"Maybe one of those top producers you have stashed in the back in one of those cages would like to learn a new trade."

"Are you smoking dope or what? Those people make more while you're doping off at the water cooler than you make in a year."

Water *cooler?* He always *did* exaggerate.

"I rest my case," I said.

"So what do you want me to do?"

"I don't know. Try the zoo. I hear you can sometimes find an elephant who will work for peanuts."

"Very funny."

I don't know what made me so cocky. There was a big fee at the solving of this case, but this was an impossible case.

I bid him adieu, telling him, "I just have to have this time or I'll wind up in a psycho ward."

"I've been saying that's where you belonged," he snorted.

And you provided it for me at your feet at Elbert A. Wemple and Associates, Realtors, I thought, but didn't say.

After I hung up the phone, Wiggy asked me, "Who was that?"

"Oh, just some guy I used to work for."

"But you're trembling," she said. "Why?"

"Yeah, well, maybe I'll have to work for him some-day again."

"Why in the world would you work for someone who makes you tremble—just talking on the phone?"

"Good question," I admitted. "In life we are not always given a lot of choices."

"Speaking of choices," she said, "how about some ethnic food?"

"Oh? What kind?"

"Ethiopian."

I made a face. "I don't even know where Ethiopia is."

"If you like the food, I'll take you there sometime."

It was such a charming offer, I didn't think twice.

My first mistake, because the next thing I knew we were sitting on the floor of an Ethiopian restaurant being served an assortment of mush, which tasted no better than it looked.

"So where *is* Ethiopia?" I asked my well-traveled companion.

"North Africa someplace," she said. "Haile Selassie—something to do with the Italians in World War II."

"The Ethiopians were probably trying to get the Italians' food."

Wiggy lapped up the mush with the slabs of some-thing that looked like pita but not as good, thoughtfully provided in lieu of saner utensils. Her taste buds must have been on a hiatus. While I watched her eat, I decided the time was ripe as an old tomato to try out my Tylenol syndrome.

"What do you think of this?" I asked her. "We're all running around trying to nail a guy who believes in The Seven theory. What if the bomber just made that up to throw everyone off? Remember the Tylenol poisonings? A guy did it at random to cover up murdering his wife with cyanide-laced Tylenol. So, here a guy wants to kill one of these guys, for whatever reason, so he starts to kill others to

60

make us think he's a conspiracy crank."

"So, why drag in The Seven?"

"Maybe it was getting too hot for him and he thought he could deflect interest to someone else. Or, is it a different guy?"

"It's a game with a lot of them," she said. "Some want to get caught. Some get their kicks from killing, some from evading capture, some from leaving their signature on the crime."

"The FBI—swimming in the resources, could be ensnarled in their own bureaucracy and their corporate mind could just be dead wrong."

"So should we give up looking for a conspiracy crank?"

"Not yet. You start here and work your way up the coast with your writing-a-book ploy," I said. "You know we have all these mythical profiles and we don't know a thing about him. Where he lives or *how* he lives. Nothing! Maybe you'll talk to someone and something will break."

"Yeah," she said. I was doing most of the talking because Wiggy was doing most of the eating. I must admit, when I was with her, I never suspected she was the killer. That only came up when we were apart.

"Tomorrow, I'll take the shuttle to the Big Applesauce and hit the last three targets."

"Who are they?"

"Ludwig Duesberg, Chairman of the Foreign Relations Council; Frank Smithson the mutual fund wizard; and Harold Mattlock, the media mogul." I didn't plan to see Mattlock. I just threw him in to throw her off.

"Those guys will see you?"

I nodded.

"I'm impressed," she said. "Say, did you ever think it might not be such a bad idea—popping some of these over-bearing bores?"

"No." Was she serious?

"Well—it's just a thought," she said. "Or maybe one of The Seven is doing it because he wants to rule the world alone."

Dessert was offered. I politely declined. Rice pudding crushed to pulp by a dozen barefooted Ethiopians did not whet my appetite.

On our way out, people were spilling over onto the sidewalk to embrace this *haute cuisine*, there being absolutely no accounting for tastelessness.

Next morning, Wiggy took me to the airport, and we kissed at the curb—I with a desperate passion befitting my paranoid fear of flying. Every kiss at an airport could be my last.

I had made telephone appointments before I left—all the doors of the richest, most powerful men were open to me. The only trouble I had getting an appointment was with my son. He was awfully busy and it was such short notice he'd need a shoehorn to squeeze me in—and he couldn't promise a time. He would be coming from an audition, "And you *know* how unpredictable they can be," he said. Of course, I didn't know, but I took his word for it.

Somehow the plane took off, stayed afloat and as we landed I noticed the two World Trade Center buildings looked like smokestacks. Then, I sat back in a taxi with a Russian driver, for the most dangerous part of the trip—from the airport to the headquarters of the Mayflower Mutual Funds in lower Manhattan. The driver apparently had it in for the KGB.

Frank B. Smithson, the mutual fund wizard, with enough funds under his control to pay off the national debt saw me in his office, high above the hoi polloi in the Wall Street section of the over-sized apple.

He could see from his perch, the World Trade Center smokestacks. Just to remind him of the efficacy of bombing.

Smithson was perhaps the youngest of the remaining targets, somewhere in his early fifties. He wore rimless glasses on a face that looked too young for glasses. His trim body was covered with a gray, pin-striped suit off the rack of some traditional clothier. His office was he-man stuff with dark paneling of Brazilian rosewood which has been embargoed for decades. He-man brown leathers covered the furniture, even his desk which was the size of an airstrip in a one-horse town.

I didn't realize it then, but he was perched atop a sixty-some story building which was entirely devoted to his enterprise, the Mayflower Mutual Funds.

"Perhaps the most surprising thing," he said to me after we were seated across the airstrip from each other, "is this didn't happen sooner."

"Why is that?"

"The disparity between income classes in this country is continually widening. With all the poor, it's not surprising there is going to be resentment."

"But murder?"

"Why not? It only takes one crackpot to bring this kind of thing off—what do we have—280 million or something? No," he shook his head, "I'm just surprised there aren't more nuts around."

He was a bookish looking guy in his no-frame glasses, like you might picture a guy with a passionate interest in some genus of butterfly. But he knew his numbers. He was always speaking of mathematical percentages and I suspected that understanding could have been the secret of his success.

"Sure, I *was* worried," he said, "for a day or two. That's as long as I am able to worry about anything. If someone wants to kill you, they don't usually talk about it. Ninety percent of the things you worry about don't happen. The other ten percent happen whether you worry or not; so why worry?"

"Do you think this bomber's view of you is justified? That you have so much money you are ruling the world?"

"No," he said. "People misunderstand. We have giant mutual funds, yes, with trillions of dollars invested in the market, but we are talking about hundreds of companies and millions of investors. That's where the money is—not in my personal hands.

"I am not one of the richest people in the country. I

don't aspire to be. I have more now than I spend, so my keeping at it has nothing to do with making more money. It gives me something to do. I don't feel old enough to suck my thumb on world cruises.

"And," he added reflectively, "if this guy has his wish, I'll never get that old."

"Are you acquainted with all the men who are supposed to make up The Seven?"

"I don't think I ever met Ludwig Duesberg," he said. "I know the others from slightly, to well."

"Who do you know well?"

"Gideon Golan and I were at Yale together," he said. "We still keep in touch. He's in town or I'm in Washington, we'll go to lunch." He chuckled, as if to himself. "I can imagine if one of these cranks sees us, he'd think we were plotting the future of the markets. Rule the world!" he said, shaking his head.

All these guys seemed to scoff at the idea. Protested it, really.

"Could there be such a thing as you seven having such a tremendous influence on things that it amounted to you having the fate of the country in your hands—I mean, without any overt actions to make it so?"

"No," he said.

"I mean, the Federal Reserve Board does set interest rates. You benefit from that. I suppose preknowledge of what the board was going to do could make you billions."

He shook his head. "If it were just Gideon and me, you could have a point. But there are thousands of mutual funds, thousands of stocks and bonds, and millions of people in the markets. For every buyer, there is a seller. Everybody knows when the Fed meets. With interest rates they can do three things; raise it, lower it, or leave it alone. There really isn't that much mystery about it. A lot of factors go into their decision. We are all aware of those factors. We aren't often surprised. Every action of the Fed is discounted in prices before it happens. And Gideon doesn't *know* before the meeting what will happen. They vote. Majority rules.

Besides, Gideon is a pro. He would *never* talk about what they might do. We don't talk shop when we meet."

"Did you know any of the bomber's victims?"

He nodded, gravely. "Winston Chambers of the CIA, I met at a party once. That's all. Of course, our funds have blocks of stock of United Motors and Softex. But so do hundreds of others."

"Did you know Carlisle of United Motors? Or Bob Fenster of Softex?"

"Not well. I knew them both socially, when we would be thrown together at some charity affair or other. Fenster didn't go to many of those, but I did meet him a couple times to talk about his stock."

"To see if you wanted to buy it?"

He nodded. "Or sell it."

"Did you do one or the other?"

He nodded again. "Yes. We have quite a lot of it. It's been very good for us."

"You ever sell it?"

"Some, but we're into Softex for the long haul, as of now."

"And United Motors?"

"More apt to be cyclical. We'll buy and sell, as we think the market indicates."

"Ever sell either short?"

"We have only a few funds that do short sales. I don't think Softex was ever sold short, though I'm not sure. United Motors I know we have sold short in the past."

"What about Harold Mattlock?"

"I've seen him now and again. Seems like a good guy," he said. "I think he works a lot harder than I do—flying all over the world and what have you."

"Have you ever wondered if anyone was out to get you?"

"Not before this guy," he said.

"If you had to produce a list of people who might want to harm you, how would you go about it?"

He parted with a lugubrious chuckle. "I suppose, a

list of our fund holders who lost money. Checking them out could take a couple lifetimes."

"You mean everyone doesn't make money?"

"Hardly."

"For every winner there's a loser?"

"Essentially. The loser may not actually lose on his purchase, but if it goes up after he sells he will consider himself a loser. So the part the buyer gains, he loses."

"Always?"

"No. I'm talking about stocks and stock funds. Flexible instruments. We have funds like CD funds, government-bond funds which are primarily for the interest they pay."

"Can you think of a reason someone could and would kill the seven of you?"

"Pure crazy paranoia."

"Nothing you could stretch your imagination to besides random insanity?"

"I'm sorry," he said, "I honestly can't think of anything with any rational basis."

After I left him, I wondered why I was uneasy about Smithson. I once heard DeLorean speak at a small theater in Palos Verdes. He had been tried for drug dealing and acquitted, even though the Feds had a video of him in the transaction. He gave a lovely talk, telling how he'd found Jesus and was railroaded big time by our G-men in action. He was persuasive—the quintessential salesman, and I was convinced. I, who scoffed at conspiracy theories, was willing to accept DeLorean had been the victim of one. But something bothered me. In all his shining ninety-minute talk, he never once admitted he ever did even the slightest thing wrong. He was perfect. Too perfect.

That's how I felt about Frank Smithson.

9

My second cab ride in New York, from lower Manhattan to midtown, brought home to me how silly it was to fear flying. For here, on the surface of the earth in New York, was the real danger. My fate was in the hands of a maniac, native-born, with eyes the color of cheap crack cocaine and a grudge against anyone who challenged his space—said space being every inch of the street, as far as the eye could see.

I haven't any idea how I arrived alive at the squat building on the East River that housed Duesberg and Associates.

All I can say about Ludwig Duesberg's suite of offices, which covered the whole floor of the building, was they were the best money could buy. A proprietary view of the East River and Golden Triangle, the celebrated professor-diplomat's corner office made a believer out of the most skeptical.

When I raved about his views, he said, "Ach, if I look out da vindow, I get noting dunn."

Duesberg seemed settled into a calmer existence than his hectic years in the limelight as secretary of state. Though his posture was stiff, perhaps owing to a perceived deficiency in vertical inching, Ludwig Duesberg seemed fairly down-to-earth—if you could seem down-to-earth being a fugitive from Nazi Germany without leaving your thick accent with *der Führer*.

He treated me as an equal, as much as that was possible, for a guy whose IQ must have been triple mine. He sat us in what he referred to as, "my zitting room," a stagy collection of stuffed furniture with blue and white patterns on them like Wedgwood china.

He told me his wife decorated the place. His current wife, of course. "The first one vas no decorating sense."

When I asked him about the bomber, he said, "Oh, dat is crazy. Whoever sez to put me on dat list, is chust plain crazy. It is men with billions of dollars on dat list. I don't belong dere. Ven I vas secretary of state, I haf much more power dan today. I haf a nize conzulding business here, sure, but da chairman of da Foreign Relations Counzil is not as impordant as being president of der Rotary Club."

I ticked off the names of the other six of the unlucky seven, and asked if he knew any of them.

"I know dem all except Golan. He came to Vashington after I left. He vas a banker before dat. Out vest somewhere—maybe Chicago. I don't know him." Duesberg's eyes scrunched in thought, pulling visions from the past. "I knew Winston Chambers, da CIA ven I vas in government. Many meetings—not any about ruling da worlt."

"What about?"

"National security," he said and winked at me. It was the catchall disclaimer. "National security." He pronounced it, "see-guridy."

"Harold Mattlock I knew liddle bit. See him at doze awful functions ve seem to go to against our desires." He looked at me over his glasses and threw out his hands. "Vat are you going to do, dey tell you it is for charity and dey lay on you deze guilt trips."

"Did you know Bob Fenster and Phil Carlisle?" I asked about two of the three victims he had mentioned.

"Dey are clients of mine. Vell, dere companies now. I represent dere interests abroad. Ve never once all got togeder at da same time, let alone made any plans to rule da worlt." He snickered at the absurdity of it all. "Dat shows you how liddle people know. As if it ver possible to rule da worlt—or dhis coundry—or Cheyboygan, Michigan, for dat matter. Schtoopid! Schtoopid!"

"Are you worried?" I asked.

"Nah—ven I vas secretary of state yah, den I vas sometimes vorried. Now iss crazy. Of courz, da police an da FBI haf sed up elaborate protections, but I am not a young man. It vud be quick. Much better dan canzer."

"That's an admirable attitude," I said.

"Nod enough life left in me to spend it vorrying abaud some insane cragpot."

I left him my message number, and he said he would be glad to call if he saw anything unusual. But I had the feeling I would not hear from him.

Having some time to spare until the best-case meeting with our son August, I decided to walk crosstown to our meeting place in the theater district. I also thought it would be safer than taking a cab. And I had the feeling I was right about that while I was on the sidewalk. Crossing the street was another matter. Those crazies who drove the cabs now had you for a target. And you were unprotected.

New York, I decided, was definitely not my cup of hemlock.

I harbored a secret admiration for our "wayward" son. Here was a guy who knew what he wanted, what gave him pleasure in this vale of sniffles, and he went after it, in spite of the odds and the snickers.

Daddybucks thought he was an aberration. "I defy you to point to the slightest genetic warning that my family would wind up with a male ballet dancer!" Code for it must have been *my* family's gene pool that baptized him.

August was just one less guy who would be suffocated by the omnipotent, the omnipresent, omniflabby thumb of the great repressor himself, Daddy Pimple Wemple.

We met (his choice) at one of those grungy delis in the heart of the heartless theater district. He was working me in between an audition and his stint as a clerk at one of those discount bookstores with two names.

For maximum fat, I leaned toward pastrami at these delis. I think you are definitely better off to have something that was cooked along the way, preferably cooked a good, long time.

Since I was not consulted, Dorcas dear and Daddybucks Wemple named our son, August Wemple Stark, after that quantity lard product, Elbert August Wemple. I felt sorry for the kid, because there was virtually nothing recognizable you could do with the name. Augie and Gus weren't bad, but Wemp was too much like Wimp. Nothing ever took, so he was saddled with August, like he was some flaky Roman emperor or something.

One thing about ballet dancing, it kept you thin. And August was always fit as a viola.

He was a good-looking blond kid—about 5' 10"— surprisingly never plagued with acne; good bones, nice proportions, body and face. If you asked me, I'd say that was more startling, genetically speaking, than becoming a dancer.

"How'd the audition go?" I asked as he hustled into the narrow deli with his duffel bag slung on a shoulder. In that section of the Big Applesauce, storefronts rented by the front-foot. So you had a lot of places that were about eight-feet wide and three-miles deep. The best tables were those you could reach without falling over from heat exhaustion.

"I was pleased," he said. "Trouble is, *they* have to be pleased, so you're always on pins and needles."

We made our way to a table, a distance of what some years ago would have constituted a summer vacation.

When we sat, he put his duffel bag on the floor at his feet, and said, "I ran into Greg at the audition—I asked him to join us when he finished—I hope that's all right. I haven't seen him in ages."

I waved a hand, as though I was one blasé dude. Actually, I was a little disappointed that my son wanted a buddy along for our too-infrequent meetings.

"Is everything all right with you?" I asked, making hay while waiting for my son to shine.

"Can't complain," he said.

"You have a new job, don't you?" I asked.

"Yeah, four months," he said. "I had it up to here waiting tables," he said, slicing his throat with his forefinger. "People drove me nuts."

"Bookselling is better?"

"Yeah, I guess. Pay's the pits, and you still get your share of kooks, but it's lots less stress. How about you?" he said. "Everything okay?"

"Apricots."

"Peaches, Dad. That's supposed to be peaches. Peaches and cream."

"I'll try to remember that," I said.

"No you won't," he said. "Oh, here's Greg"—and he seemed to light up more at the sight of Greg than he had for his own father.

Greg slid in the chair next to August. They smiled, touched, rolled their eyes and raised their eyebrows, as they relived the audition and catted about some of their competition.

The waitress dragged herself to the table, as though under some internal protest. She took out her pad and wet her finger, then applied it to flip to the appropriate page.

That was, she made clear, the sum total of the communicative effort she was willing to expend in our behalf. I ordered the pastrami with everything; August and Greg agreed to split one of those concoctions recommended by Anorexics Anonymous.

I tried to bring Greg into the conversation. Though what I was doing, was trying to bring myself into the conversation.

"What do you guys think of this conspiracy bomber?"

"The Seven guy?" Greg said. "Creepy." I'm not sure August knew who we were talking about. He never seemed too taken with murder and mayhem. "Who were the victims?—Fenster of Softex, of course. The CIA guy, and who was the other one?"

"Philip Carlisle—United Motors."

Greg shrugged, "Big, rich, powerful guys. Maybe that's a risk you have to take."

"You think so?" I said. "Random killings?"

"Aren't random," Greg said. "Anything but. Very individual—targeted."

"You think there could be something to the idea seven people ruled the world?"

"I've heard crazier stuff," Greg said.

"You?" I asked August.

"I won't go for any number of world rulers unless fearless Elbert August Wemple is among them."

I'll say this for the kid, he knew how to win my approval.

"Made a lot of enemies," Greg mumbled.

"What's that?"

"Some of those guys made a lot of enemies. Take Fenster. Stepped on a lot of bodies to get where he is. There's a guy *I* could believe ruled the world."

"Why?"

"The corner he has on the personal computer-software market. Stepped over a lot of dead competitors to get there."

"You don't mean they killed people literally?"

"I don't have any firsthand knowledge, no, but I know a lot of competitors were ruined along the way."

"How do you know all this stuff?" I asked.

August answered. "Greg's a computer nut."

"Oh?" I said.

"Yeah," he blushed, as though he were being accused of something both undeniable and scandalous. "Yeah, I read a lot of stuff, I guess," he shrugged in half-apology. Then as if in justification, he said, "Computers are taking over the world. Look at how pervasive they've become in a handful of years."

"So, tell me about Bob Fenster, will you?"

"You mean you don't know about him?"

"Only in the vaguest sense," I said. "I know he's sort of a whiz kid and very rich."

72

"Both sublime understatements," Greg said. "He was an M.I.T. dropout," he snickered. "What could they teach him? He could teach *them* plenty, but he had bigger fish to fry."

"Remember that one, Daddy," August said. "Bigger fish to fry. It's a good one. Lot of possibilities like broiling a big salmon."

"Okay," I said. "I'll try. So then what?" I asked Greg.

"He starts this software company—calls it Softex."

"Like Kleenex?"

"Not much—just the name. Now don't forget, we are talking about just under twenty years and he's already the richest man in the country. He didn't do that letting grass grow under his feet."

"Right place at the right time," was my contribution.

"Way more than that," Greg corrected me. "Lots of guys in software, but they all lacked something he had."

"What?"

"Some lacked his genius. And I know that word has been devalued by overuse. But Bob Fenster *is* a genius in *any* sense of the word—was," he corrected himself, as though he had trouble getting used to the idea. "He has—had, a way of cutting to the chase—putting his finger on what's important—what's needed—what's saleable. And he's single-minded, driven, doesn't care about money—he's just a super-nerd."

"*Was*," I corrected him.

"Yeah, right. What a shame. Part of us all died when he did. You have any idea how all-pervasive his influence was in the world? Still is?"

"I guess I don't."

"He's in everything. Just think about all the computers running the world. Well, he's responsible for running almost all of them."

"What were you saying about him doing this over a lot of bodies?"

"Well, that's the other thing about him. Nobody

gets in his way. And the competition along the way didn't roll over and play dead. He had to roll them over. A young kid like that isn't going to be worth eight to ten billion without ruffling a few feathers."

"Yeah, I guess."

"But it's a real tragedy. He just got married—built a huge house."

"But you aren't surprised somebody killed him?"

"No. When you are so successful and so beloved in some quarters, you are bound to engender the opposite feelings in equal magnitude."

"Do you know anything about the other victims of this latest bomber?"

"Nah. Just Fenster."

"Nothing that would tie them up?"

"No, except that it is virtually impossible to live in the world and *not* be tied up with Bob Fenster. If having ties to him and his product was the criterion for killing, you'd have to nuke the whole country."

We finished our sandwiches, and I left Miss Congeniality a tip commensurate with her charm and grace.

I thanked Greg for his information, and asked if I might call him if I had more questions.

"I'll keep in touch with August," he said. "I move around a lot."

My son and I hugged briefly, and I thought I put a little more into it than he did.

August and Greg disappeared down the street. They seemed quite content to have put me behind them. The only thing that salved my feelings was August had not asked about his mother.

10

I called Harold Mattlock from a phone in a drug-
store on a corner. He wasn't in. I left my name and asked to
have him call me back in Washington at the Hay-Adams in
five or six hours.

A Pakistani drove me to the airport. He seemed to
be in some kind of religious trance, and he drove as though
guided on automatic pilot by some higher being.

After a bit of telephone hide-and-seek with Harold
Mattlock, we connected and he agreed to use his best efforts
to get me an interview with Jennifer Fenster. It was a day
and a half before he was able to produce a telephone number
she agreed to answer.

"I must have been crazy to tell Harold Mattlock I'd
talk to you," Jennifer Fenster said to me on the phone,
Washington, D.C. to San Jose, California. "I don't know
anything about it. I still haven't gotten over it."

"Would you be adverse to contributing to catching
the killer?"

"Well, no," she admitted. "Certainly not, but I
haven't cooperated with anyone. For two months, I was a
basket case. I was in a virtual coma. Catatonic. I had married
the greatest man in the country, and suddenly—Wham
Bang!—no more."

She sniffled into the phone, but when pressed,
agreed to see me, if for nothing more than to supply a little
background that might help solve the case.

My antennae were vibrating. Jennifer Fenster, all things considered, sounded believable. So why the vibration? It happened at two points of the conversation. The first was—"I was a basket case...in a virtual coma. Catatonic." It sounded like overkill—and then, "Wham Bang!—no more." Was she protesting too much?

I thought Wiggy should do some research about the relationship of The Seven to Bob Fenster and the other two victims. She wanted to go with me to San Jose.

"I'm not turning you loose on any rich widows," she said.

"How do you know she's rich?"

"Are you kidding? Fenster was worth around ten billion."

"You don't think they had a prenuptial agreement?"

She seemed stymied. "I guess they must have."

"Check it out, will you?"

"You've given me quite a load," she said. "You aren't trying to get rid of me, are you?"

"No—but our time is up—the bomber may strike again. Any day."

Wiggy claimed not to like San Jose, and agreed to do her work from San Francisco—where we would meet after my talk with Jennifer Fenster *in situ*.

Jennifer Fenster was not one of those young women who put on the high heels and mascara to go to the workplace where she wanted to be treated like a man. For the high heels tightened and sculpted the gluteus muscles with just-so provocation, and the mascara made the eyes sparkle with eager longing—neither characteristic of much use for the serious striver in the work force.

Immediately, I could see she was a woman who moved with purpose: who could cover a lot of ground with her energetic stride. Bob Fenster wasn't the only person in the crowd who was driven. But Jennifer had the knack for tempering her ambition with the shield of femininity. She had the rare ability for smothering her designs in common-sense concern for the pleasure of the patsy.

She had brownish hair that fell pell-mell to her scapulae. When she walked, her hair took on a waving motion like the surface of a calm, but deep, sea.

She wore a pink suit that looked soft as cashmere. I didn't touch it, of course, but you could tell it was top-cabin goods. Underneath the jacket, she wore a plain-white pullover blouse and a strand of pearls which were definitely not the mock.

As we sat talking in her living room, I couldn't shake the feeling that we were in the Colosseum—in Rome, not Los Angeles.

There are in this rarefied social strata those with commodious houses, big houses, oversized houses, grand houses, and incongruously grandiose houses. The Fensters' new pad was larger than all of them. After I saw the size of the place, I kept looking around for a golf cart to take you from room to room. It wasn't that one would be too lazy to walk the house, it was just that it would take too much time.

And this, I noted, from Bob Fenster, a man who reputedly had trouble parting with a nickel—before he was married.

Jennifer and I settled into north- and south-facing couches respectively. The seating was hewed from the skins of some very young, and obviously adorable, animals.

"What was it like," I asked, "dating the richest man in the world?"

She smiled—as though she weren't sure she should *be* smiling. "Much like dating the poorest, I suppose."

"No, weren't you, well, scared?"

"At first, I'm sure I was. Then I realized he started out like all the rest of us—with somebody changing his diapers. And he was such an innocent, really. You've no idea. But when a man devotes himself to success with a single-mindedness that blinding, he really *can't* see anything else."

"*Was* it success he was devoted to?"

"No, I think not. It was ideas—making the best mousetrap. The field was so new, so challenging, and he took to the challenge like what would you say? A mouse to cheese? No, no—a duck to water."

I threw out my ineffectual arms indicating I was the wrong person to ask about clichés.

"Some girls thought Bob was this giant nerd. That was the lipstick and mascara crowd. Well, maybe he did fit some definitions of a nerd, but nerds don't like to be reminded of their nerdiness. Besides with Bob climbing so high in the world, that was really a moot point.

"Lots of girls set their caps for him around here. That's normal. Not only was he the richest, most successful man in the country, but he had never been married. Never been touched actually. It's what I call the feminine domestication urge. We see a guy footloose and fancy-free, and we think it's a kind of patriotism to get the harness on him. It's a badge of honor for a woman. And Bob Fenster, as you can imagine, was the Congressional Medal of Honor."

"Is that sort of what you thought?" I asked nerdily.

She allowed herself the luxury of a suddenly truncated laugh. "I could never admit to designs that cold and calculating. No self-respecting girl could," she said. "But just as surely, no self-respecting predator anywhere in the magnetic field of Bob Fenster's boyish charm could resist the pull of the challenge. And those of us lucky enough to be admitted to the very limited circle of his presence became either stupefied or silly."

"Which were you?"

She laughed again, then cut it suddenly as though it were inappropriate. "A little of both, I expect."

"Which did he prefer, stupefied or silly?"

"Hard to tell. He'd seen so much of each."

"So, how did you get to be the lucky one?"

"Oh," she said, her eyes darting away from me for a moment, "I still wonder about that. All that occurs to me is I genuinely cared about him and he could tell. Bob had a knack for smelling out the phonies. It was a big reason for his success."

"But surely, there were other girls who cared for him?"

"I suppose—but when you have *that* much money, you are especially leery. It's like you're always looking over your shoulder—afraid you'll be mugged by some gold-digger. You are bound to be suspicious of everyone. I guess I allayed that suspicion better than most. And I was in *marketing*. And fairly successful at it. Everything is a product to be sold. A candidate for matrimony is no exception."

"So, how did you go about selling?"

"Just like anything else. You analyze the market, and you analyze the product, find the fit, and go for it."

"But there must have been a lot of competition."

"Not that much, actually," she said. "Of course, I'm not counting aspirations. Everybody had aspirations—but you needed access, as well. Bob Fenster was introverted in the extreme. Nobody, but *no*body came between him and his monitor screen."

"So, how did you get the opportunity to meet him?"

"I worked my way up in marketing. I started right out of college."

"Where did you go?"

"To college? You dub," she said, and I was confused. I thought she was calling me some kind of new-age dummy.

"You dub?" I asked. "Is that like, you dumb?"

"The University of Washington," she said, smiling the smile Bob Fenster couldn't resist.

"Oh," I caught on. "U and part of double-U. Great," I said. "How many people in marketing?"

"Hundreds," she said.

"So, how did you get to even meet him?" I asked. "Was it like that saying, oh, what is it? The milk falls to the bottom or something?"

"The cream rises to the top."

"Is that it? It's so hard to remember with all the milk being homogenized."

"I worked my way up until I was in charge of projects that got Bob's personal attention."

"Bob—you called him Bob then?"

"Everybody did. Softex is a first-name place."

"Did you think while you were working your way up that you might marry him?"

"No girl, if she's being honest, would deny at least some thought of that—but most of us would consider it little more than pleasant fantasy. That's the way I looked at it. It wasn't a calculated thing. I didn't set out to grab him. It was just too remote. I didn't even know him."

"But you must have known about him?"

"Sure. Rumors. He's driven, he's brilliant, he's *the* world-class workaholic. He probably never even *thinks* of women. When would he have time?"

"So how *did* you bring it off?"

"Yeah," she said, as though amazed at herself. "People tell me I should write a book on how to nab a rich man. But it wasn't like that. It really couldn't be and be any good. You are marrying a person, not a pile of money."

"So how did it happen?"

"I don't know. There was this instant chemistry, I guess. We just both went 'Wow! Where have you been all my life?' When that happens, you aren't thinking money. And, if it doesn't happen—the chemistry, I mean—the money isn't important either."

"But there was so much of it."

"Yes, but don't forget, Bob didn't spend any of it. He didn't have time—he wasn't interested in anything but his beloved computer software."

"But, some say you changed all that."

"Oh, they give me too much credit. I didn't change much, really. Yes, I tried to convince him that money in the bank was essentially worthless—that he should do something for himself—and get it working in the economy. So, I asked him if there wasn't anything he'd like to have—anything he'd ever thought about *before* he was so rich—and he said he'd like to have a house. So, we built a house."

"Did you ever!"

She laughed again. "You certainly are making me laugh," she said. "More than I have since..." she hung her head, "...since he...died."

"Were...you with him...when he...died?"

She shook her head. "I was here—he was at the office. It was a special delivery package—marked 'personal' with a return address he recognized. It was some computer disks he thought—something he had been expecting. And when he opened it—" she stopped with a gasp.

"Do you know what the return address was?" I was trying to tread gently.

She shook her head. "His secretary knew. The FBI checked it out. It was one of his software developers—he worked at home. The bomb wasn't from him—obviously. You don't send a bomb with your own address on the package. Imagine opening a package that said 'Bomber' on the upper-left-hand corner." She shook her head again, more dolorously. "Pete Ryba was the developer. He's been through hell with the FBI, and he is just devastated someone would use him like that."

"Did they get any leads from him?"

"No," she said. "He gave them everyone he knew, but it was obviously not someone Pete knew, but someone who had found out Bob was expecting mail from Pete."

"Did it ever come?"

"Yes—later the same day."

"Do you know anything about this conspiracy theory that seven people rule the world?"

She shook her head.

"Never heard anyone espouse the theory?"

"Never heard of it," she said. "First time was when I read it in the paper. That murderer is crying out for attention. Imagine anyone doing such a thing—three times—and then telling everyone why." She shuddered. "Imagine anyone so crazy!"

"I wonder," I said, "remember the guy we called the Unabomber?"

She nodded. "How could I forget? That was a fear

we never really got over. He was killing people remotely connected with technology. Who more connected than Bob? But he didn't get him. Then this copycat comes along."

"But there were the other two—United Motors and the CIA. I don't see the technology angle. Not in the CIA anyway. So, it's similar, but no carbon cat."

"Carbon copy—copycat," she muttered.

"Any big enemies?" I asked. "Suppose someone wanted to kill him, and the other two were cover-ups?"

"Lot of trouble," she said. "But enemies? Who doesn't have them? But Bob was the most easy-going guy you could imagine."

"How much of his business dealings were you privy to?"

"Very little before we married. Almost everything after."

"Am I wrong, or wasn't there some animosity over an antitrust thing—or a merger or buyout or something?"

"All of those things," she said.

"Any of them bad enough to kill?"

"I don't think so. I don't see people in that strata murdering people. Sure, feelings run high—some people are mad as can be when they lose these things—but killing?" She shook her head. "With this kind of cunning precision. That takes a special kind of nut, don't you think?"

"Yessss—but we can't leave any rocks without turning them over. Maybe, one of them would have an idea that would lead to something."

"Well, maybe."

"Investigation is all persistence—following the remote leads in hope that one will lead to something."

"If you say so—" she said.

"Yeah," I said, casually. "If you could give me some names—I could start."

She sighed, not the sigh of the put-upon, but rather of one who has suffered hopelessness once too often.

My footsteps reverberated like shells in the FBI shooting range as I left the cavernous home of Jennifer

Fenster and the late Bob Fenster. I was armed with a bunch of names of people Jennifer knew to be less than taken with her late husband.

All right, I'll admit it. I was smitten with Jennifer Fenster. She was beautiful, unaffected, friendly and a lot of other stuff. But can you ever overlook a spouse in a murder? She hadn't given me anything that might incriminate her.

But, then again, why would she?

11

Armed with Jennifer Fenster's list of competitors and the name of the Softex man-in-charge, I drove into downtown San Jose, and checked into the De Anza Hotel on Santa Clara.

On the way I passed a passel of palms: *Trachycarpus fortunei,* the Chinese windmill palm; *Syagrus romanzoffiana,* the queen palm; *Phoenix canariensis,* the Canary Island date palm; and the *Washingtonias*—the shorter, fat-trunked *filifera* and the tall, skinnier-trunked *robusta.* The *filifera*— American cotton palm, a.k.a. the California fan palm—is the only palm native to the United States.

Like a lot of western cities, San Jose began as a small town where they planted seeds and ran some livestock. One thing led to another, people having a way of reproducing, and the village leaked a flood of over a million souls. Houses and more houses marked the flatland until this laid-back Los Angeles was the third largest city in California—larger than the early leaders—fabled San Francisco, and beleaguered Oakland of which Gertrude Stein said, "There is no there there." In San Jose there is a there there, and it's everywhere.

The De Anza Hotel was a human-sized enterprise, beautifully appointed, competently run, and reasonably priced.

The front entrance of the hotel was graced with pots of *Chamaerops humilis,* the Mediterranean fan palm, on either side of the doorway.

Inside under the desk was a glass etched with a cycad leaf—*Encephalartos lebomboensis* is my guess.

Over the elevator, etched in glass was a complete cycad plant—something like *Encephalartos cycadifolius*. But probably it was just the artist's rendering of the more common *Dioon edule*.

The offices of Softex Micro Computers was just down the street. My room on the seventh floor overlooked the parking lot where many of the employees parked their cars. I could monitor their comings and goings.

Looking out the window, I saw Señora Emma's—a wide horseshoe of a sign with a woman from her elbows up with skin as pale as a Dutch maiden. She seemed to be holding a tray of beer glasses, only the beer was green. Later, I discovered the green beer was actually cactus.

The stucco building was milk chocolate with mint-green trim and out front were six forlorn queen palms—was this a town for palms or what?

In the distance—at the end of the flat downtown, was a hazy mountain stretching the distance of the horizon. Down on the side of Santa Clara Street, flags waved in the light breeze—United States, California, Mexico, and San Jose. Across the street stood a high bell tower that perched atop an office building as though it had been transferred there from some Mexican country church.

As soon as I was settled, I put in a call to Wiggy, who had told me she would be staying at the Huntington Hotel on California Street atop Nob Hill.

She wasn't in. I left a message.

I planned my next moves for my morning at Softex—Wiggy didn't call. I had a lot of thoughts about what she might be doing. None of them good.

As a diversion for my naggingly suspicious mind, I turned on the television. There I came face to face with that familiar grimness of the newscaster giving us the calamities of the evening. The countenances are stern, but there seems to flow beneath the public tragic mask, the undercurrents of satisfaction. Satisfaction at having a startling and gripping lead story to pump up the ratings.

It was with a ghoulishness worthy of the happiest of Halloweens that the anchor of chance (the one who popped up when the electronics gelled the screen into life) announced that the Unlucky-Seven Bomber had struck again. "Gideon Golan, chairman of the Federal Reserve Board died instantly when he started his car in the garage of his home in Georgetown. Chairman Golan is the fourth victim in a series of grisly bombings reputedly committed by a disaffected crank who thinks seven people are ruling the world and should be stopped. Other victims have been Philip Carlisle, president of United Motors; Bob Fenster, founder of Softex; and Winston Chambers, head of the CIA. The remaining three of the alleged seven are Harold Mattlock, media baron; Luddie Duesberg, chairman of the Foreign Relations Council; and Frank Smithson, chairman and founder of the Mayflower Mutual Funds. That particular order taken from the list of The Seven supplied, allegedly, by the bomber himself. If it is accurate, that could mean Mattlock is next. More after this," and there was a rapid and grateful cut to a commercial, some creatively edited, slam-bang pitch for automobile security systems. A wave of nausea swept over me. Gideon Golan was such a nice man. And he was big enough to admit his vulnerability. What kind of monster could do such a thing to such a good man?

When we returned to the entertainment portion of the news program, the head ghoul sent us skipping across the country with the miracle of electronics to solicit the opinion of friends, colleagues, and kin of the unfortunate deceased rendered even more unfortunate by this maudlin display of mawkish sentiment.

We were treated to a cousin's lament over this terrible tragedy—the immediate family had the sense to decline the numerous interviewer proposals, then a colleague speculating on what this might do to the stock market. "Hard to say; I'd speculate on an immediate decline on tomorrow's opening, but I would also expect a timely correction."

"Would it be fair then to say you don't expect any long-term effect on the stock markets due to this unfortunate tragedy?"

"That's correct."

That was an interesting coupling of words, "unfortunate tragedy." I wondered if the commentator had ever experienced any *fortunate* tragedies.

Unhappily, the remaining content was on a similar intellectual plane. Skateboarding the other channels yielded no better. Even the president of the United States weighed in with a pledge that all the law enforcement agencies at his command would be mobilized, full strength, to combat further terrible tragedies, and to solve this heinous crime.

I was disappointed there had been no opportunity to question the president with one of those "How-does-it-feel?" questions—"How does it feel to be president of the United States and the titular head of the free world and not be considered important enough to be in the seven most attractive bombing targets?"

The phone rang. It gave me the perfect excuse to turn off the set. "Hi, Wiggy," I said in a voice I now realize carried the overtones of inebriation.

"Mr. Yates?" the baritone intoned, and I knew it was Harold Mattlock.

"Yes, sir."

"This is Harold Mattlock."

"Yes, sir."

"Apparently you were expecting someone else."

"Oh, yes, sir," I stumbled, "an associate on the case—doing research. I didn't know you knew where I was staying."

"Yes, we tracked you down. Not that many hotels in San Jose," he explained. "You saw the news?"

"Yes, sir."

"Nice the way they remind everyone who is left. The remaining targets, so to speak."

"The news, sir," I said, stupidly. Harold Mattlock *was* the news.

"Don't I know it," he acknowledged, "and putting me first..." he trailed off as though there was no more breath in him. "Any progress?"

"Progress, certainly," I assured him.

"But no solutions?"

"No, sir. It's been a matter of days."

"Yes, and who knows how many of those precious days are left to us."

"Well, sir, he has taken his time between...victims."

"Depends which side of the equation you are on. It doesn't seem so long to me."

"I understand."

"Do you think we should put more people on it?" he asked.

"That's entirely up to you."

"Do you think it would help?"

"I don't see it hurting," I said.

"What would you say about the fee?" he asked. "I mean, I have no need or desire to cut you out of your fee if someone else reaches the result we want—but I understand you are not that kind of small-time operator. Either you produce or you don't *want* to be paid. And let me tell you," he ran on without giving me a chance to protest, "I admire you for it."

"Thank you, sir."

"But let's say I do try to add some troops..."

"The hundred thousand will be satisfactory," I cut in.

"Well, I..."

"If you want to pay less," I said, "perfectly all right."

"Quite big of you, Yates."

"But, I will be pulling off the job."

"That does seem a bit drastic..."

"Not getting paid seems a lot *more* drastic to me."

"Yes, yes, I can understand. Can you give me any kind of update on your activities?"

"You mean, so you can pass on my legwork to someone who can close the deal?"

"No, no—I'm just curious what you've been doing."

"All right, I've interviewed all the survivors. Chairman Golan was a real gentleman."

"Yes."

"As you all are."

"That's comforting."

"I've attended a meeting of a coven who buy this seven conspiracy. I've gone over the FBI data, and I'm researching various relationships in The Seven and working on some angles which I can't relate at the moment."

"You're in San Jose. I guess that's going all right? You saw Jennifer Fenster?"

"Yes, sir—thank you for setting that up."

"My pleasure. Any good from it?"

"Too soon to tell," I said. "She's been cooperative."

"Well, keep me posted. You can imagine this puts us further on edge—my wife, my colleagues, employees, stock-holders."

"Yes, sir. Does that mean our original fee agreement is still good?"

"What? Oh, the fee. Yes, yes, sure."

12

The next morning Wiggy still didn't answer her phone. I left another message.

Kenny Irving, the new president of Softex, was too busy to see me in the morning, but he graciously made a spot for me in the early afternoon.

So, I called Teo Erosky, Fenster's former partner who "retired" to a four-hundred-acre spread outside of Los Gatos.

"Sure, come on over," this folksy voice said on the phone. "I'm not doin' anything. Glad to talk to you." I didn't know if that was the voice of regret or the voice of contentment.

I followed his directions in my rental car. The air was clear and snappy, and the rolling hills en route were most pleasant to behold.

Fencing four hundred acres could be a gargantuan task, but Teo Erosky was one of the five or so richest men in the world. And he didn't work! So, we are talking in the billions, and out of that fortune, Teo Erosky bought himself a lot of fence. Far as the eye could see, as far as I could see.

I pushed the button at the gate and identified myself, whereupon the gate swung open and I drove in. Then, I drove and drove—could it have been two miles?—to the comfortable-looking, low-slung adobe ranch house that couldn't have taxed the imagination of any scrub-league architect. It was big, but it looked like Erosky could have built it with his own hands.

He came out the door to greet me before I got out of the car. He was a stocky guy with hair all over the place. He was simply, almost shabbily, dressed. And if he had been thinner, you might have mistaken him for a homeless guy.

He was the antithesis of all I read about Bob Fenster—his partner in the creation of Softex. He was so laid back I wasn't sure he was altogether awake. But he was as friendly and unpretentious as anyone you could imagine.

"This is a unique house you have here," I said.

"Thanks," he perked up. "I built it myself."

"You did?"

"Yep—adobe clay and straw. Made my own bricks. Got a lot of time on my hands since I left Softex."

"Why did you give it up?"

"The rat race? I made so much money, I started to wonder what it was all about. A guy like Bob Fenster could keep going indefinitely." He shook his head. "That's not me," he said. "That's not to say I don't admire him for it. Bob was the driving force. I was just sort of along for the ride."

"Oh, I doubt that."

"No, it's true. We did start the thing together, and I guess I was as gung-ho as he was in the beginning, but the thing got so damn big and all-consuming, I didn't know which end was up. So, I bailed out with my bunch of stock which over the last ten years or so turned into billions. Well, come on in the house," he said, and he led me through a rough-sawn-plank wood door into his adobe hovel that was dark and dampish. Windows were a lot harder to make and place than a bunch of adobe brick, apparently.

In the living room, we sat in furniture I could only characterize as crude, and you guessed it, he made it himself. He wasn't going to run off with any craftsmen prizes, but he did take a hand in creating his own environment.

"Like a glass of water?" he asked.

"No thanks."

"How about a cracker or something?"

"No, thanks, I'm not hungry."

He smiled—a sheepish kind of grin—"Cracker wouldn't be much help if you were," he said.

"Do you ever wonder—if you hadn't left Softex—if you might have been the target for one of these bombs?"

"Crossed my mind," he said.

"Any ideas?" I asked.

"About the killer? Nah. Have to be some real crazy. I mean, think about it. What does Bob Fenster really have in common with the CIA or the FRB?"

"How about United Motors?"

"Well, at least they have some of our software—thin as it is, it's *some* connection."

"Is that a big account?"

He nodded. "Huge."

"Does the FRB use any of your stuff?"

"Everyone with a computer uses something. You can hardly escape the loving arms of Softex. But the FRB has to be negligible," he said. "So does the CIA. The FBI has more of our stuff than the CIA and FRB combined."

"Maybe if J. Edgar Hoover were still alive, the FBI would be one of the targets."

"Maybe. I can see some nut thinking the FBI might rule the world. The FRB chairman, no way," he said.

"Do you have any thoughts on The Seven theory?"

"Seven guys rule the world?" he said, shaking his head in amazement. "And not one of them is president of the United States? Something is screwy."

"Any theories?"

He shook his head. "I can't make any sense of it. Only the media gives these things such a blast, it seems one nut strives to outdo the other on these serial killings. It could just be a megalomaniac looking for a way to get noticed."

"A little extreme," I said. Then he shrugged. "What was it like working at Softex?" I asked.

"A pressure cooker," he said, easily. "There is a constant fear—spread from the top—that if we let down for only an instant, we could lose everything."

"Fenster you mean?"

He nodded. "Bob was unique, to say the least. A more single-minded, devoted guy I couldn't even imagine. His life was his work, and vice versa. I mean, he didn't devote two seconds' thought to anything else."

"Well, he got married, didn't he?"

"Yeah—to a woman in the company who was granted a lot of face time."

"Face time?"

"Yeah, that's what we call it, face time with Bob. Meaning, you see his real face—not just some message on the computer. And don't forget, he was over forty years old when he allowed himself that luxury. But Jennifer is a top marketer, so I'm sure there wasn't any time wasted on dates talking about furniture or silver patterns."

"What if she tried it?"

"He'd be thinking of something to do with the company."

"They built a house."

"*She* built a house," he corrected me. "And his devotion rubs off or you are rubbed out of the corps."

"Happens?"

"Sure, it happens. Oh, Bob took pride in being a benevolent boss—and he was. You wouldn't be fired if you burned out—you just wouldn't be promoted. If you were already up there, you'd see your face time with Bob dwindle to zip. Funny thing," he chuckled. "Bob built this great recreation facility for the staff. They call it 'The Resort'—but everyone's afraid to use it. Don't want to be seen doping off. So all the tennis courts, the swimming pool, the golf course—empty." He shook his head.

"And what was Bob Fenster like—personally?"

"Well, I grew up with him, you know. He was nerdy I guess, so was I. Always tenacious, bright as a whip. His genius is knowing the market and how to play it."

"The stock market?" I asked.

"No, no. The software market. He's a marketing

genius, as well as a programming genius. He knows what's needed, what will sell, how to sell it."

"And how to make it so the competitors are locked out."

He nodded. "There's that too."

"Might that rile some of the competitors?"

"I expect it would."

"Enough to want to kill him?"

"Well, I certainly don't know anyone like that—but I have been out of it for ten years."

"Spend any time with Bob Fenster since you split?"

"Some," he said. "We were still friends. I was on the board of directors—but it's all different if you don't share his goals. Especially now that he got so big. He was like a gunman from the Old West who's got endless notches on his gun—he was always looking over his shoulder or keeping his back to the wall so someone didn't take him by surprise and knock him off. But what kind of life is that? You can't let up for a minute. You can't bend over to smell the flowers for fear you take the fatal one in the back."

"That what he was like?"

"Yeah, well, *was*. No more. He had nine, ten billion bucks. Where did it get him? I have three or four billion, I don't even know how much, the numbers are so big. So I'm out of the rat race and so is he. Only I can still smell the flowers."

"Does his death affect you at all financially?"

"Oh, I don't know. I expect it will in time. There was only one Bob Fenster. Another shall not pass this way soon—so I expect the stock will drop some in the long run. But so what? You know a billion is a thousand million. I could lose ninety-nine percent of my stash and still come out with thirty to forty million. Think you could get by on that?" he asked me.

"I imagine," I said.

"Well, so do I."

"How about enemies?"

"Well, hell yes. You don't get that rich without stepping on a few toes."

"Like who?"

"Anybody who was dumped on. Anybody who had his dreams crushed by the colossus."

"Anybody stand out?"

"In what way?"

"Any way: displayed anger. Anyone who was irreparably ruined. Anybody frustrated beyond their capacity to endure it?"

"You know, if you're looking for a guy who could blow up all these people, I don't think I could help you. See, I don't believe we're dealing with a rational human being. Not someone who could have achieved what was necessary to go toe-to-toe with Bob Fenster in the first place. The kind of guy who's big enough to go up against Bob Fenster's colossus is not the kind of worm who mails people bombs."

"Last one was in the guy's car."

"Yeah," he snorted. "Make him a higher type worm, you think?"

"Maybe lower. Maybe a different killer?"

He shrugged off offering an opinion.

"You know Kenny Irving?"

"Yeah."

"I'm going to see him this afternoon. What kind of guy is he?"

The shoulders bobbed up again. "A good guy," he said. "Devoted. Some say he's a Fenster clone. I don't see it. He's driven, ambitious, tireless for the company, but I think he's missing that X-plus."

"X-plus?"

"Yeah—that certain hidden ingredient that sets the geniuses off from the good guys. As I said, there was only one Bob Fenster. *Could* only be. We won't see the likes of him in our lifetime."

13

Teo Erosky was a guy who seemed to have found the key to living. If your bent was toward dark adobe houses, isolation and uncomfortable furniture. Maybe being out of the rat race had its drawbacks.

Kenny Irving was a coin of a different feather altogether. As soon as his statuesque secretary opened the door to his office, I saw this was one driven cookie.

As can be imagined, Kenny Irving was the record holder for face time with his predecessor, Bob Fenster. He was calm and friendly on the outside, but I could imagine inside he was another kettle of angry crocodiles.

He was tall and thin, kind of handsome—but he didn't maintain his physique by strenuous exercises—he didn't have time for anything except walking briskly to and from his car: one of those sleek Ferrari things that idled at a hundred miles per hour. And Kenny Irving idled at the same speed. He kept his weight by not eating. It wasn't that he didn't like food, he just couldn't find the time for it. He stayed alive popping salted peanuts into his mouth at idle moments.

I thought it interesting that Teo Erosky offered me a cracker, but Kenny Irving didn't offer me peanuts. Doubtless, it would take too much time.

Kenny wore casual clothes, as did everyone at Softex. An open-neck, knit, purple polo shirt and some khakis just like Humphrey Bogart used to wear.

His office was reasonable size, but he wouldn't be giving any fancy-dress balls there. It wasn't big enough, or fancy enough either. It did look down one of the main streets in San Jose and caught the mountains at the horizon.

He sat at his desk, I across from him. Behind him was the latest state-of-the-art computer.

We got right down to business. "Anyone you can think of would want to kill Fenster?" I asked right away. I could tell the prez would want it that way.

"Depends," he said. "I can think of numerous people who have had murder in their souls after we knocked them out—but I can't think of one of them actually capable of murder."

"Or hiring it?"

"A hit?" he looked perplexed. "So elaborate? With the other victims? That's not hit work, that's derangement."

"What about inside the company?" I asked. "Anybody angry enough—had an agenda that would benefit from removing Fenster from the picture?"

He shook his head. "We all worshiped Bob," he said.

How nice, I thought. *Too* nice. "Any nasty rivalry to replace him after he died?"

"Not nasty. Spirited maybe."

"Would you say his death benefited anyone in the company?"

"Just the opposite," he said with reassuring emphasis. "This company *was* Bob Fenster. We all know that. I can work twenty-four hours a day, all my life and not accomplish half the things he did."

I tried to detect a hint of pique there without success. "Was there any financial benefit to anyone when he died?"

"Some of us got increases in salaries, bonuses, stock options. I suppose I got the most, but I don't have time to spend anything."

"Are you married?"

"Yes."

"Your wife have time to spend?"

He grinned. "She finds the time," he said.

"Have you been with the company from the beginning?"

"Almost. A few months after they got together—Bob and Teo—a little over twenty years now."

"What was your position back then?"

"Position glamorizes it. We were all scut workers—did what needed to be done. Sales, programming, personnel, administration, advertising. Whoever had five minutes got the next project. Those were exciting times."

"More than now?"

"In a way. We were poor, dumb kids, operating by the seat of our pants."

"Things more structured now?"

He grinned. "You could say that. In those days all that was at stake was our pride. Now—" he spread his hands, "we are responsible for thousands of people, and it weighs heavily on us."

"You think Teo made the right decision?"

"Getting out, you mean? It was the right decision for him. I'm afraid I'd be bored silly."

"I take it along the way you've had a lot of battles with competitors. Lot of bodies in your path?"

He nodded, gravely. "Inevitable," he said, as though he were making a reluctant admission.

"Any stand out as the turning point for the company?"

"Lot of turning points," he said.

"All of them turned you up?"

"Most of them. We've had our disappointments."

"But you are the most successful company in the country today, wouldn't you say?"

"I've heard that said," he said.

"Do you agree?"

"Well, how do you measure success? Money? Sales? Average compensation per employee? Stockholder equity per capita? Profit?"

"How about market domination?"

"Share," he flinched. "Market share we call it. I suppose we have been fortunate in that."

"That what it was, good fortune?"

"Some," he said. "Our best fortune was to have a leader like Bob Fenster."

"So, why would someone kill him?"

Kenny Irving shook his head. "Crackpot," he said. "Have to be insane. I guess these nuts get a rush out of eliminating someone so much better—more important—than they are."

A disturbing pattern was emerging. Everyone said the bomber had to be a crackpot. There is an old Chinese proverb that came to mind. "Whenever two people agree, already there is trouble."

"Could you give me a list of people you've had to beat to get where you are?"

"I could try," he said. "Be a long list."

"Okay," I said. "I have a pen."

He started twenty years before with their first coup. He gave me names, incidents, and his assessment of the damage done to the competitor when the smoke cleared.

It *was* a long list.

While I was scowling at it, Kenny Irving shot a fistful of peanuts into his mouth.

"What kind of things do you do that could make your competitors angry?" I asked.

"You name it," he said. "I can imagine how utterly frustrating it would be to go against a company as competent, prepared, and savvy as we were."

"You say that in past tense?"

"I do. We'll still give it the old college try but..." he spread his hands again, "it's just not the same without Bob."

"What are some of the unfair practices you are accused of?" I asked, trying another tack.

"The usual," he shrugged. "Monopolistic control, overpowering with our clout in the industry, fixing our applications and operating systems so certain others work with ours, while others won't."

"Any truth?"

"Some," he said. "Always a germ."

"Do you fix your software to eliminate others?"

"Do you understand software development?"

"Not at all."

"Well, it's not really that simple. Sometimes you set out for effects you don't achieve, and sometimes to achieve effects you didn't set out for. We don't try to eliminate the competition through development practices, we try to be the market leader through superior products."

"And does one thing lead to another?"

"Well, our size and success would seem to lead onto more success, and the more successful we become the harder it is to compete with us. That's natural. But Bob was always terrified it would all come crashing down on our heads if we didn't keep plugging. We had to continue to be in the forefront in perpetuity. He never tired of reminding us what happened to IBM."

"What happened to them?"

"They fell off their pedestal."

"How?"

"Got complacent," he said, throwing some more peanut fuel into his furnace. "Some years back the government got the hots for breaking up monopolies. They settled for that go-round on AT&T and IBM. Turned all their guns on those two companies for years. Then, for some reason, they let IBM off the hook and concentrated on AT&T. Well, you know they broke up the phone company, and as a result AT&T prospered. But IBM, who they left alone, disintegrated. Their business went to hell and so did their stock."

"Is the government after you?"

"All the time."

"And you prosper from it?"

"I wouldn't say directly," he said. "But it keeps us on our toes. Bob never let us forget the lesson of IBM."

"What about the other victims? Could they have had any other ties to Bob Fenster? The CIA, the Federal Reserve Board? United Motors' Phil Carlisle?"

"I don't think Bob knew any of them personally, if that's what you mean. United Motors was a big customer—the CIA and Federal Reserve Board—I'm afraid I'm not up on government—or anything outside the job, for that matter. I have a vague idea what the Federal Reserve Board does, but I don't know what the CIA does when we're not at war."

"Is there anyone in the company that might know more about Bob Fenster's relations with these guys?"

"I don't think he had any—but let's see—you know, I can't think of anyone. I've been here longer than anyone who is still left, and I had more face time with Bob. He never mentioned anything. I'm ashamed to say, I don't even know who these government guys were. I know the president and my senators and that's about it."

"So, you go through life pretty much with blinders on?"

"Yep, focused on the job. Have to, if you want to survive in this hyper-competitive market."

"Bob Fenster was like that?"

"Are you kidding?" he said. "Bob Fenster was the prototype."

Quietly, I said, "But he didn't survive, did he?"

Kenny Irving stared at me in a way I thought must have blurred my image in his eyes. He threw a handful of peanuts into his mouth, as though he didn't realize he was doing it.

"Good point," he said.

14

On my way back to the hotel, I passed some more palm trees. *Washingtonia robustas*—but San Jose is too cold for most of the twenty-seven hundred or so palms. The *Washingtonias* reminded me of home, and I was glad the city mothers planted them. I didn't know what to make of the peanut-popping prexy. I couldn't see him setting off any bombs, even if it meant elevating him to the head of the most successful company in the nation. But I was beginning to wonder if one of these super-nice people wasn't *too* super-nice. Could I have already talked to the murderer?

Back in the room, the red dot was lit on the phone, indicating I had a message.

It was from Wiggy. I called her. And miracle of miracles, she answered.

"Geez, Wiggy," I said, "where *were* you?"

"Where *was* I?" she riposted. "I was running my buns off in your behalf."

"All night?"

"You bet your sweet patootie," she said.

I didn't know what a patootie was, but I didn't ask.

"You don't get results sitting on your behind."

"You mean you *got* results?"

"You bet your sweet patootie."

"Well..."

"Well, what?"

"Aren't you going to tell me what they are?"

"On the phone?"

"Why not?"

"Too big," she said. "Too scary. I've got to see you in person."

"Well, geez, I..."

"Don't you *want* to see me?" she said with a slinky voice that purred. "*All* of me."

Oh, yeah, I did. "Where?" was all I got out.

"Here," she said.

"But, Softex is here."

"Yeah, but your answers are here—in Frisco—with my heart."

"What's that?"

"The song—don't you know it? *I Left My Heart in San Francisco*. Well, so did I, only I'm still with it. Huntington Hotel on California Street," she said. "Top of Nob Hill, short for snob."

I was on my way. I took a couple cookies from the lobby desk when I checked out—to fortify me for the trip.

San Francisco is one of those places you are better off without a car. But since Harold Mattlock was still sporting my expenses, I decided he could afford to park my vehicle wherever they did it.

Wiggy opened the door in one of those sexy, filmy, cream-colored, robe-like things that were not made with privacy in mind. And before you knew it, neither of us had much privacy.

Her suite had a view of the city to the ocean, but we weren't looking at it. And was *she* sweet! The first thing she said when she opened the door was, "I have so much to tell you, I can hardly wait." But, we waited, and fascinating as her news was, I'm not sorry we digressed. She really was an exquisitely sexed human being.

It took some luxurious moments to get our breathing under control. Wiggy disengaged herself with the exception of her lone right arm which she left under my neck. We were side by side on our backs on a most accommodating bed. She was staring at the ceiling, I was staring at her.

"So, what did you find out?" she asked.

I told her of the names of possible disgruntleds I'd gotten. "It's quite a long list," I said.

"How many names?"

"A couple dozen or so," I said. "But some seem more likely to be ticked off than others. What did you find out?"

Now she turned her gaze from the ceiling to me. "I started poking around about Winston Chambers—the CIA guy. He was from Frisco you know?"

"No, I didn't."

"Yeah. A federal judge before he was named top spook. You want to guess what one of his cases was while he was on the bench for the Frisco circuit?"

"Somebody versus Softex?"

"On the money, honey."

"Don't tell me," I said, holding up a hand like a school-crossing guard. "Softex won."

"Yeah, but that's only the beginning. You know what Gideon Golan was in *his* former life?"

"No."

"A banker..."

"And he loaned money to Softex?"

She was nodding vigorously.

"And Carlisle at United Motors was a huge, early customer for Softex products," I said.

"Yes, and Luddie Duesberg represents Softex abroad, and Frank Smithson's Mayflower Fund is very heavy into Softex stock—largest single stockholder outside of the company."

"And Harold Mattlock has gotten fat off Softex advertising."

"Well..." she said, "he was pretty fat financially to start with."

"Yeah, sure, but we're talking perception here. What some nut sees."

"Now, all we have to do," she said, "is find that nut." And she gave me a thoughtful and competent hug.

"Let's look at your list," she said.

I dragged myself out of bed and stumbled around the living room until I came to my senses and turned on the light. Wiggy was right behind me, as I rifled my brown-leather briefcase for the papers. Both of us had been too preoccupied to dress.

I laid the list on the desk and we both peered at the cold, black handwritten scrawl that formed the names, hoping, I suppose, that a name and circumstance would pop up and hit us in the face.

"Which of these guys was on the other side in the Softex case that Chambers had?" she asked.

"I don't know," I said. "What was the name of the company?"

"Something called Program Art."

My finger passed down the list until it rested on Victor Nulty...and behind it Program Arts.

Wiggy and I looked at each other without either of us noticing the other's nakedness.

A delicious euphoria swept over us. "Victor Nulty," we said simultaneously.

When we came back down off the ceiling, we sank into a sudden depression. "What now?" Wiggy asked.

"Let's do a little analysis here. Put yourself in the guy's place. All his life's ambition down the drain to this colossus. The dreams—pft! The labor—splat. A lifetime goal not only unrealized, but ruined for all time—"

"Why couldn't he come back? Try something else?"

"Because Softex was growing so big they were virtually untouchable. The ideas were all being pursued by a billion-dollar company. If he could hire a thousand guys, he'd still be left at the starting gate. So, he decides, what the heck, I'll just blow everybody up—everybody that had anything to do with Softex. That could be quite an order. The way they tell it, there aren't many people in the world that *don't* have something to do with Softex."

"Well, there's four less of them now."

Then we argued about how we would approach

Victor Nulty. Wiggy wanted to go along in the worst way. I thought two-against-one would be like ganging up on him. Intimidate him into reticence.

"Okay," Wiggy said. "Then I'll go alone."

"*You?*"

"Why not? You know about Sigmund Freud, don't you?"

"The boy, girl stuff, you mean?"

"Go to the head of the class."

"He could be homosexual," I offered lamely.

"Oh, Gil, *really*! What chance is there of that? And if he were, what would *you* do about it? Enter into a relationship with him...?"

"No," I said, "but—are you saying you would?"

"Don't know," she said, matter-of-factly. "Haven't seen him yet. If he's as cuddly as you are..."

"No, no, sorry," I said. "I can't let you sell your soul to the cause."

"Soul? Who said anything about *soul*? We're talking body."

We argued some more. Then she said, "Okay, I'll arm wrestle you for it."

I was struck dumb. "What's the catch?" I said at last.

"No catch," she said. But there had to have been. Surely I was stronger than she was. Not that I was a world-class arm wrestler or anything, but certainly men are stronger, physically, than women...generally, anyway. But what experience did Wiggy have arm wrestling?

"You some kind of champion at it?" I asked her.

"No," she said.

"Know some special tricks? Have a lot of experience?"

"No."

"Just—think you're stronger than I am?"

"Could be," she was looking at me askance.

I was in a quandary. I certainly didn't want her going alone—it was *my* case after all. But I didn't want her tagging along, either. Not only did I think it would inhibit Victor

Nulty from opening up, it would also smack of unprofessionalism. Confidences, when they flow at all, flow one-to-one.

"Okay," I said, with a macho air that made me *feel* macho, "you're on."

Like mere mortals with a larger purpose, we rose and made our heroic ways to the dining table the Huntington Hotel had thoughtfully provided for our vital activity. The sunshine was giving San Francisco an amber glow and here I was, Tyranny Rex's insignificant other, high above the mélange of structures vulnerable to earthquake, fire and flood, not to mention pestilence and greed, and I was looking down on it. I felt invulnerable.

Then I sat at the table diagonally across from Wiggy and put up my right paw.

"Let's do it left-handed," she said.

"You're left-handed," I said, and we argued about that for a while until I no longer felt invulnerable. We negotiated our disagreement to a best-two-out-of-three, right hand, left hand, then flip a coin for the hand we would use for the tie breaker.

When we joined hands, my first thought was tenderness and romance. It was a mistake, Wiggy suddenly had me inches from the tabletop—the wrong way. I struggled and sweated, gesticulated and grunted until we were as straight up as the Transamerica Tower, where we seemed to be at a standstill. All I could think at that moment was if she could do this with her right hand, I had no chance with her left. I heaved and hectored that pretty, strong hand until I sensed a slight weakness. Then I summoned all my strength for the kill and moments later she collapsed. I was surprisingly proud of myself for winning a test of strength with my right hand against the right hand of a left-handed woman.

She glared at me and put up her left hand, erasing all doubt that I might have harbored about her letting me win. But I couldn't allow her to win. Even if she *were* stronger than I. I couldn't send a woman alone against a psychopathic serial killer. Just because I may be in the forefront of the affirmative action for the women's movement, doesn't mean chivalry is dead to me. I may not have been Olympic material in arm wrestling, but I was not without adrenal glands and I was calling on them now as never before.

Cautiously, I raised my left hand, it was no contest, she had me flat down in less than a minute. I may have had the glands, but the adrenaline was slow in coming.

We flipped the quarter. Heads we agreed would be right hand, tails, left. The coin flipping hit the table then dropped off onto the floor. It was heads.

"No fair," Wiggy said. "It has to land on the table."

"We said no such thing," I argued.

"It's just understood," she said. "Rules of the game."

"Ridiculous," I said.

"*Not* ridiculous. Suppose it had gone out the window, would that still count?"

"Oh, Wiggy—really."

"No, we're going to flip it again. This time I do it and it has to land on the table or it doesn't count."

"But we didn't agree to that before," I protested again, but she had taken the coin and tossed it gently in the air, and it landed in the center of the table.

"Heads."

And so it was I got to visit Victor Nulty, solo.

15

Victor Nulty was in the phone book. It was a business named CSC—Computer Software Consulting, and when I told him (he answered the phone himself) I wanted to consult on some software problems, we made an appointment.

His appointment calendar seemed relatively clear because I was invited to meet him in his apartment/office, an hour later.

Victor Nulty's apartment was near the Tenderloin district—in the rump of the tenderloin you might say.

For my dollars and sense, the Tenderloin district of San Francisco is one of the most aptly named sections in the country. Entering it requires a Dantesque descent from any part of town. And once you're down there, you feel down—there. And you don't get up until you're out. With the slew of sex shops, strip joints, sex shows, even the toughest loins start to feel tender.

As I sashayed through the sleaze, I thought what a peculiar venue for a software consulting business. As I began to climb out of the slough into the residential rump I was surrounded by clapboard two-story houses—as though anything higher was or would be brought down by an earthquake. Those structures only startled in the earth shaking, were still in use. The residence/office of Victor Nulty was one of those.

En route to Computer Software Consulting, a couple guys asked me for loose change, but all my change was as tight as I was, so I held onto it. I considered making suggestions about their career choices, but my intuition told me they would not be receptive. It seemed to me in their line of work they would have done better in the financial district. But here, in the rump of the tenderloin, was home and verily it is said, home is where the loins are.

I climbed a number of wooden steps, which over the years had had the sap kicked out of them, and reached the door with the plastic tag that said in a quiet but majestic manner:

Victor Nulty
Computer Software Consultant

The door had been freshly painted baby blue, as if for my visit.

I knocked beside the door, afraid I'd get a knuckleful of baby blue. After a decent interval, the door opened and I was facing a guy about my height (a modest inch or so under six feet) with a careful smile on his well-lined face. The lines were in cowhide, not silk.

He was a bald, scholarly looking man who had not been weight-watching for some time. His apartment seemed to reflect his plight: cluttered austerity. The clutter was not priceless antiques, but stacks of *Wall Street Journals,* printer paper, company reports, studies and reams of software-speak. His computer was in the corner, behind his desk.

"Cleanliness and order are the sign of the mundane mind," he said with a wry smile. And, true enough, he did not show me a mundane mind.

He invited me to sit at his desk facing him. The clutter of papers thereon served to mask some of his avoirdupois. We chatted about his credentials and he guilelessly told me his history, beginning with his meteoric ascent in the stratosphere of software, to his rapid lunge into bankruptcy. He unabashedly blamed it on Bob Fenster, and Softex. "Lost everything," he said, "business, house, car, wife, kids. Even the dog was taken from me." He never tried to hide how sorry he felt for himself.

"Fenster did all that to you?" I asked, my head swiveling in wonder.

"He certainly did," he said. "That guy was a hero to a lot of people who didn't understand his crushing, megalomaniacal business *modus operandi*."

"Yeah, I suppose any guy who gets that rich has to step on a few toes."

"Stepping on toes is one thing—crushing the body—quite another."

"How many companies have gone under...?"

"All of them. If there are any competitors left, it's just a matter of time and—wift!" he snapped his fingers to portray a disappearing act. "But enough of my past, what can I help you with?"

"Just that," I said. "And your present."

He frowned.

"Don't worry," I said, "I will pay your fee for the time."

"But why do you care about all this?"

"I'm what you might call an amateur detective," I said, and I could see the skepticism in his eyes with my eyes closed.

"Really," he said, with a flat disdain.

Victor Nulty consulted his watch, not, I think, because he had another appointment, not because he wanted the session to end, but rather to see how much fee he had earned.

"How did you get interested?" he asked.

"Read the papers. The Seven-conspiracy idea intrigued me."

He smiled as though I had praised his first born.

"That was a terrific idea," I said.

"Yes, wasn't it?" He was smug. He was self-satisfied—and *so* forthcoming.

"You are to be congratulated," I said.

"Me?" He looked surprised.

"It was your idea, wasn't it?"

He looked at me a long time in silence, then sadly

shook his head.

"But you've just about admitted it," I urged him on. "Oh, don't worry, I'm not a policeman."

He nodded as though that thesis was not hard to accept.

"So, how did you bring it all off? I'm dying to know," I said, without realizing I might be putting ideas into his head.

He stared at me awhile longer and I began to squirm under the apprehension that he was sizing me up for a concrete wet suit.

"So, your premise is I had a motive, so I killed him?"

"Well, did you?"

He sized me up some more, and apparently saw nothing threatening in my size.

"Wouldn't you have?" he said. "Think of it. Here is a completely selfish megalomaniac who is not satisfied to be the richest man in the world, and preeminent in his field, he has a maniacal compulsion to destroy all his competitors.

"So, you're his main competitor, back when it was still possible to compete with a colossus. Your life's work, as well as all your dreams are wrapped up in applications for the automobile industry. You have done superior work and the giants have been preoccupied elsewhere. You are about to get a contract that will set you up for life. And don't misunderstand, this isn't me alone I'm talking about—there were hundreds of us involved. Venture capitalists breathing down my neck. Yeah, I know about that guy, he got bombed, too. Not only did he call our loans and sink me into bankruptcy, but he made Softex their early loans. He was big in lending to software companies.

"So, anyway, Fenster and Softex snuck around behind our backs and made a deal with United Motors."

"A better deal?" I asked.

"Of course not." He spoke to me as he would to an amiable mental deficient. "They didn't have the technology on this application. They were playing catch-up."

"So, how did they do it?"

"The usual," he said. "Industrial blackmail. Stick with us because we're in everything. We'll make you a special deal on all those other applications of ours you are using. Early access to betas versus waiting for released product. You get the picture. It's not a pretty picture, but it works. If Fenster had his way he would control the world."

"The software world?"

"Oh, no, he wouldn't be satisfied with that, once it had been achieved. He'd move in on the Internet, cable TV, regular TV—soon you couldn't drive a car without paying Bob Fenster a licensing fee." He spread his hands apart. "So you see, he had to be killed."

"So you killed Carlisle at United Motors."

"He was...removed for reneging."

"What about the CIA man?"

He nodded. "The judge who threw the case to Softex."

"Why did he?"

"Blackmail and bribery."

"You really think they paid him off?"

"What other reason would there be for ruling for Softex? It was a monopolistic maneuverer no matter how you slice it. Blackmailing United Motors—threatening to make them *last* in the industry to have Softex applications if they didn't accept the Softex setup instead of ours."

"But, couldn't someone else supply what Softex did?"

He shook his head, tersely. "Too entrenched. A gargantuan task. Probably the computer software industry would come crashing down while they tried to catch up. No," he shook his head again. "Same as Softex trying to catch up with us. It took them two years and what they got still wasn't as good as ours."

Computer technology was not my sack, as they say, but I was catching on. Softex was everywhere. Victor Nulty gave me chapter and refrain of the inner workings of the industry, and, as with so many industries, those who get there first have incalculable advantage. Softex set the standards, then when they were inextricably entrenched, they altruistically shared the standard so that other companies would have to wed their stuff to a Softex component. The end result was Softex had to be everywhere. All they left were the crumbs."

Taking this confession was like depriving a minor child of his sweets.

"What about the bombs? Could you do that?"

"Make them? Are you kidding? Any schoolboy with a science magazine or access to the internet or a library can find diagrams showing exactly how to build a bomb."

I always thought my naiveté was a strange advantage in my bizarre avocation. Now, I wasn't sure, because Victor Nulty squinted at me and said, "Surely you know that."

"You put three bombs on target," I said, more in awe than in question.

He nodded as though fatalistically.

"How could you do that?"

He smiled.

"I mean, you got Fenster right inside the company— how could you bring that off?—and even got *him* to open the package. I don't imagine he opens many packages himself."

"He doesn't open any, anymore."

"Did you...I mean, didn't you feel any remorse?"

"What, when he blew up? Not a bit. I was in ecstasy."

"How did you get it there? In Fenster's hands?"

"Now you're asking too many secrets," he said smiling, I thought, ruefully. I mean, here is this guy who was a certifiable monster admitting all this stuff to me. But he was looking at me in a way that said—what are you going to do about it? Like a challenge. Like now that I know it, all he had to do was give me a third eye socket, without the eye. He knew it, I knew it, and he knew I knew it.

So, now I figured my immediate goal was to get out of there alive.

"Now what?" he said. "You going to the cops?"

"What for?" I asked.

He nodded. "I'd never admit it to the cops," he said. "And you have no proof."

"Right," I said. "Well, what do I owe you?"

He looked at his watch, padded the bill a little, and I paid him. "Oh, by the way," I said, looking around the place, "where do you build the bombs?"

He shook his head. "I'm off the clock," he said.

I took out my wallet again. He licked his lips, but finally shook his head. I didn't blame him. That would have constituted hard evidence.

I shrugged my shoulders as though I couldn't care less and bade him good-bye.

Outside, I ducked into a convenient space between houses where I could see without being seen.

It was only a matter of minutes before Victor Nulty appeared and hustled down the street.

I followed him.

16

At first I thought Victor Nulty was headed for his bomb-fabrication facility to put together a special package with my address on it. Then I realized he didn't know my address—I breathed easier.

There were just enough people on the streets of San Francisco to provide me cover in my tailing maneuvers. We left the Tenderloin district, then climbed through Chinatown, and continued climbing the mountain that was California Street. We had passed through three areas of the Bay City: Tenderloin, Loin, and Loinless. I was catching my breath from the climb when a cable car chugged past, laden with bodies hanging on for dear life. It was just as I was wondering how they would shoehorn another physique into the soup, that Victor Nulty, across the street, jumped on the car and sped away with it.

I started to run, but with the widening gap, I soon realized how foolish that was. I looked frantically around for a taxi, but the only ones I saw were occupied. I finally found a cab in front of the Mark Hopkins Hotel, jumped in, told the driver to follow that cable car. We had caught up within four or five blocks, but by then there was no sign of Victor Nulty.

I had the driver return me to Nulty's pad.

Here is where I admire the swashbuckling private eyes who whip out their locksmith set and pick any lock in town. I also envy those guys who find the door open. If I do, I usually find myself in some kind of trap, as I did in Switzerland when I was pursuing that art con.

So instead of breaking down the door, I sought out the manager. The sign on the mailboxes said she hung out next door, and her name was Muriel Merrywether.

An elderly woman answered my knock. With any luck I thought she might be hard of hearing.

I took out my wallet and flashed my driver's license rapidly before her eyes. "Police. I need to get in the apartment next door—upstairs."

She squinted. "You don't look like no police," she said. "Let me see that badge again."

"Are you Muriel Merrywether?"

"I am—but you aren't no police."

"I'm sorry," I dissembled. "I said *please*, not police. I was just in the Nulty apartment. I left my watch. When I remembered, I came back and Victor was gone. I'm leaving town."

She squinted at me again. I felt like a penniless ex-husband begging for carfare.

"Look, you can go with me. I'll get the watch and be on my way."

"Describe it. Maybe I'll get it for you."

"Hey look—I was just in there. What's the big deal? You probably saw me go up."

She shook her head, but now I was skeptical. She didn't look like a woman who missed much in the neighborhood.

"I'll mail it to you," she said. "Leave me your address."

I shook sounds of exasperation from my head. I took my wallet back out of my back pants pocket. She had eyes on it like one of those birds with night vision. Instead of letting her inspect my license at closer range, I took out a nice collection of twenties and thrust them in her direction. "Look," I said, "that watch is important to me."

She looked from the menagerie of twenties to me and back to the twenties. As suddenly as a serpent striking she took it off my hands and stashed it down the front of her dress. I had not only given her a wad of twenties, I had given her a lopsided bosom.

She closed her door in my face, then, as I began to protest, she opened it and marched with nary more than an occasional grunt of disapproval, up to Nulty's lair.

With the deft motion of a practiced professional, she turned the key in the lock and entered, with no notice of my presence. I followed, fingering the watch in my pocket.

"Now," she said imperiously, "where is it?"

"That's what I've come to find out," I said. "I think it's in here," I said, going toward the bedroom.

"In the bedroom?" she said, casting a crooked eye at my suspected orientation. But before she could stop me, I was in the bedroom. A mattress on the floor, clothes everywhere. An unpainted dresser. Bleak, but not the slightest sign of any bomb-making facilities. The bathroom was a disaster, but there was nothing suspicious. The kitchen was completely beyond hope. Not a clean dish to be found, but no bomb ingredients either. I opened the refrigerator and quickly closed it.

"You left your watch in the refrigerator?" she said, but she didn't get aggressive thanks to her new, lopsided bosom.

I stepped from the Hiroshima kitchen to the living room-cum-office, rifled a few documents that turned out to be innocuous, then brought my hand from my pocket with my fist balled around my watch and faked plucking it from the rubble on Nulty's desk. "Here it is," I said.

Muriel Merrywether looked through me with no trouble and relieved herself of her verdict. "I'm glad you found it."

On our way back down the stairs, I tried to pump her for information on Victor Nulty. Pumpwise she proved as fertile as the Sahara Desert, until we got to her door.

"You know," I said, looking at the locus of my recent contributions, "those twenties have made you lopsided."

"So what?" she said, her eye arching.

I took out my wallet. "I just thought you might like to do some bosom balancing."

She squinted at me, "What I have to do?"

"Just be a tad sociable."

As I was inspecting another raft of twenties, she invited me in. I was sure Harold Mattlock would be good for the twenties.

When we were seated in her dark, knickknack heaven, I was transported back to the residence of Tyranny Rex Dorcas Wemple Stark, my very own wife and glass-figurine aficionado.

I searched in vain for a representation of my wife's *objet d'art,* but found instead only painted ceramic figurines, heavy on ornithology: bluebirds, blackbirds, cardinals, lovebirds, loonybirds, you name it.

There was also a complete collection of miniature football helmets representing the professional teams.

"I'm a 49ers fan," she said, when she spotted me eying the helmets. I was so pleased to know that. Professional football not being an encounter that caught my fancy. Any sport that enjoyed, as its essence, the physical overpowering of one individual by another was not, as they say, something I could relate to. Muriel, on the other hand, seemed to find something engaging in the barbarism of the sport, and its endless human collisions.

"Does Mr. Nulty like football?"

"Oh, my, yes," she said. "He's a 49ers fan too."

"Does Mr. Nulty go out much?"

"Not so much," she said, watching me rifle through the stack of twenties I carried for this purpose.

"I noticed today he walked over to California Street then hopped a cable car. Any idea where he went?"

She shook her head, but didn't take her eyes off the twenties. Buy a season ticket to the 49ers with enough of them.

"He have a lot of visitors?"

"Not many," she said.

"Pay his rent on time?"

She groaned. "That's a bone of contention," she said. "He could be more prompt. In this neighborhood you have to expect slow pays, I tell the owner."

"Ever see anything suspicious going on up there?" I threw my head in the direction of Victor Nulty's apartment.

She shook her head. "I'm not a suspicious person."

"Ever come in with boxes—mysterious packages?"

"Sometimes..."

"Ever...been to his room...after he brought in those mysterious boxes?"

"Oh, no," she answered too quickly. "I never snoop."

I nodded my head, as I was sure she wanted me to.

"Remember the last time he was gone for a while?"

She nodded as her tongue circumnavigated her lips as her eyes rested on the filthy lucre. "Here just last week," she said. "Just came back this morning."

I had more questions; she had less answers. I could tell she was trying to please me to earn herself a matching set of bosoms. Finally she asked, "Why do you want to know all this?"

"I guess you could call it a hunch," I said.

"Yeah, well, I got a hunch you're gonna go away from here and take my other bosom with you." She was frankly staring at the pile of money, and salivating in the bargain.

I pushed it toward her. I decided she had earned it. A smile smothered her face.

"There could be more," I added.

"More?"

I nodded. "You keep your eye on Mr. Nulty. Call me up if he comes back—or goes again."

I gave her my "telephone number" connecting to the phone company answering system.

"You gonna tell me why?"

I calculated the reasonableness of her request and factored in the effectiveness quotient of a person who thought their mission was bold and decided to throw her a wishbone. "Got a rich client afraid of being killed."

"By Mr. Nulty?" her eyes reached the incredulity dimension.

"Could be."

"Don't tell me...not you *too*!" she said. "The FBI was here. They've been all over it. Mr. Nulty is a little," she pursed her lips and brought her eyebrows into the pensive position, "how should I say?—well, he has these delusions. He talks about killing people—gives you all the details only it didn't happen. I think he likes the attention it gives him."

"How do you know it didn't happen?" I asked, more than a little deflated.

"I told you, the FBI checked it all out. Seems Mr. Nulty harbored these thoughts is the way that nice man from the FBI put it. Like he wanted to do these things or wished he had only he didn't. So he's come to believe he did, and he'll tell anyone who'll listen all about it."

I looked at her a long time, searching for the loophole. Was she simply protecting him? Why didn't the FBI tell me? Not significant in the scheme, I suppose.

I checked out the little football helmets, did some heavy sighing, thanked her and left.

I wasn't convinced.

17

After the downer that was Muriel Merrywether (nothing merry about *her* weather), my spirits entertained a setback. When I got back to my hotel room, there was more bad news. Harold Mattlock had sicked another investigator on me and he left a message. Naturally, he wanted to pick my cerebellum gratis and close in on a fee.

I asked him what he charged. "A hundred dollars an hour and expenses," he said, but he hastened to explain that Mattlock was desperate and anxious that this guy—one Jeremy Travers by name—did not step on my toes. Well, I had news for him. I was limping already and I hadn't left the phone.

I told him I had not experienced any big break-throughs, but I would be happy to send him copies of the FBI reports, for a more worthless pile of papers I could hardly imagine. That should set him back a couple weeks. It would take me a day or so to copy them (with the emphasis on the *so)* and I would overnight them just as soon as I could. Of course, I was *terribly* busy.

Like the good girl she may have been in a prior mutation, Wiggy beat the foliage for ex-employees of Program Arts—Victor Nulty's almost-company. She came up with quite a little list, and had started to interview on the phone a couple hunches that didn't pay off.

Together we combed the list and found three of the ex-Program Artsers working for Softex. It seemed a good place to start. They should have some loyalties that would encourage cooperation.

The peanut-popping president of Softex not only gave us the go-ahead, but set up the interviews. There were two women and one man. Wiggy took the fems—one was a secretary, one in marketing. My fella, Fred B. Allen, was one of those exceptional developers.

Next morning, Wiggy and I hit the company and went our separate ways.

Fred was a hunched-over creepy guy with bushy eyebrows who looked like he might benefit from colonic hydrotherapy. He practically had a sign on him that said "I'm your man." That's how I knew he wasn't.

When I saw him, I decided to slide into the quest. He didn't seem too pleased to have me breaking into his thought for the day. His densely foliated eyebrows tangled in a twit.

Fred B. Allen was seated at his computer screen in a darkened room somewhere midships. His wardrobe, a dark-gray suit, white shirt and solid tie, seemed to say I am plain but formal, and dressing up in a casual environment is my bid for uniqueness. The computer screen gave his skin a greenish glow, making him even more demonic looking.

"What can I do for you, Mr. Yates?" he asked, letting me know that the quicker he could do it, the better he would like it.

I told him about my assignment, my goal, my talks with his leaders, past and present.

"So, how can I add anything?" he asked.

"You can give me your take on the thing," I said, leaving a hole big enough for a battleship to slip through.

"My take?" he said. "No way did Victor Nulty do anything like it. He's a genius, and you know what they say about the thin line between genius and insanity. Well, Softex pushed him over the line." He shook his head. "Telling everybody he blew up Bob Fenster. It's sad."

"Why is he doing it?"

"I told you. He's slipped over the line," he said.

"And no wonder—all his dreams were squelched. And not by a superior idea either."

"By a superior something?"

"Sure—cunning—payola—"

"Who got the payola?"

"Who did not?"

"Judges?"

"You find that hard to believe?"

"A little."

"How much would it take to corrupt a judge? What's he make—a hundred something a year?"

"But everyone isn't motivated by money."

"No?" He punctuated his sentences with his dense eyebrows.

Since we weren't liable to agree on human vulnerability, I changed the subject. "How did you happen to make the change from Program Arts to Softex?"

"I needed a job," he said. "Program Arts went broke."

"How many people worked at Program Arts?"

"Hundreds."

"Why did Softex hire you?"

"I developed the application they were after."

"So, you sold out?" I asked, trying to shock Fred B. Allen into some damaging admission. He wasn't shocked.

"Yeah," he said. "You could say that. Except, there was no option. It was sell out or starve."

"How does Victor Nulty live?"

"*Very* frugally, I'd say. I don't know much about him anymore. Does some consulting. Last refuge of the unemployed."

"Any theories on who killed Bob Fenster?"

"Theories? Not my line. Victor Nulty didn't do it, that's all I know. Anyone else could have."

"Including you?"

"Why not?"

"Oh, fear of punishment maybe? A restrictive moral or ethical sense—adherence to the Ten Commandments. I can think of a lot of reasons for not killing someone."

"Yeah, well you haven't hit on anything yet that would hold me back."

"Can you think of anyone else who might share your permissive morals?"

"Lots. Gung-ho lot our crew was. I never saw anything like the spirit that bunch had."

"Not here?"

"Nowhere near. We're entrenched establishment here, fat from stock bonuses. There we were comers. The new whiz kids with nothing but talent and ambition; dreams. Everything on the line. We had a lot more brains than smarts. We thought excellence would win out. Well, it *went* out instead. Like a candle flame in a hurricane."

"Fenster's fault?"

"Oh, I don't know," he said, staring at his greenish screen. "Partially. But we really had ourselves to blame. We didn't understand how the game was played and we got wiped out."

"You keep in touch with any of your co-workers from Program Arts?"

"Not much."

"Two work here."

"Yeah? Who?"

"You don't know?"

"No."

"Women—one in marketing, another a secretary someplace."

"I didn't have anything to do with marketing and I never had a secretary," he explained. "This is a big place—I guess I don't know them."

I gave him their names. He said he didn't recognize them.

"How well did you know Fenster?"

"*Know* him? Not at all. Not many *knew* him."

"Well, how much face time did you have with him?"

"Pretty much in the beginning—an hour or so a week," he said. "That might not seem like a lot, but with

Fenster, take my word, it was a lot. Then it tapered off."

"Why?"

"I was bringing my project home. He lost interest after that."

"You get along with him?"

"Sure. He was pretty easygoing with me."

"Oh? I'd heard the opposite."

"Yeah, me too, but I never saw that side of him."

"Maybe because by the time you came aboard he had wiped out the competition on your project."

"Maybe."

"You say you could have killed Fenster?"

"Why not?"

"How would you go about it?"

"Never thought that far. The guy who did it seems to have done all right. So, I guess it's moot."

"Were you sorry he was killed?"

He shook his head.

"Glad?"

"That may be taking it too far. I don't remember getting any joy out of it. I didn't mourn either."

"If you were looking for the killer, how would you go about it?"

"No idea, really not my line," he said, frowning. "You seem to be doing all right. What about the conspiracy idea—the seven rulers?"

"I've heard that. Was in the papers wasn't it?"

He nodded. "And TV."

"I don't know much about it," I said. "What I read seems pretty implausible. What do you think?"

"Plausible," he said. "Lot of conspiracy buffs in the world."

"So how does this one work?"

"Seven guys," he said and he named them all without a flounder—"are so powerful they have their way with the world."

"Yeah, but I don't get the guys on this list."

"Why not?"

"Well, look who's missing. The president of the United States, for instance. He's got to be more powerful than the founder of some mutual fund."

"Smithson?" he seemed alarmed at my naiveté. "Don't kid yourself. The president of the United States is a ceremonial office. Sure he can veto bills, but if the boys and girls in Congress want it bad enough they override him. He makes a couple appointments is all..."

"Yeah, like two guys on the list, the CIA and the Federal Reserve Board."

He waved a hand to dismiss the silly notion. "He appoints them but that's it. They aren't beholden to him."

"So are you saying you *believe* in the theory of The Seven?"

He shrugged. "I'm not saying I'm personally a devout adherent, but I can understand it. A lot of other conspiracy theories are more far-fetched."

"You ever been to any of those groups that meet to talk about The Seven conspiracy?"

"Groups? I didn't know there were groups."

"Yeah. Know anybody else who subscribes to The Seven theory?"

He shook his head.

"Never discussed it with anyone?"

"Nah."

"Can you put yourself in this killer's place? He's mad as hell. He thinks everything that goes wrong in his life is the fault of one or more of these powerful men—so he kills them. What does he think will come in their place, some harmless patsy?"

"Beats me."

"A lot of the staff at Program Arts had a real thing about Bob Fenster and Softex, didn't they?"

"Oh, yeah, you could say that."

"Well, you could also say someone has killed him."

"Yeah, but you couldn't say he—or she—was from Program Arts."

"No? Well, maybe not, I don't know. But look at the

other victims—Chambers at the CIA, and Golan at the Federal Reserve. You know how they fit in all this?"

"Two of The Seven," he said insouciantly.

"But, how do they fit with Bob Fenster?"

"Oh, that, yeah, well, Chambers was the judge decided the United Motors case. Erroneously."

"And Golan?"

"The banker. Loaned Softex a lot of money."

"How about your company?"

"Yeah, he called a loan, cost us the business."

"That a good business decision?"

"I didn't think so," he said. "Apparently he did."

"Apparently. So, they're both dead, along with Carlisle of United Motors. It was that deal that brought you down, wasn't it?"

"Sure, but the other three of The Seven had nothing to do with that."

"No, perhaps not. Of course, they are still alive. But they did all contribute to or benefit from Fenster's success."

"But so did thousands of others."

"Not so high profile." Then I added what I thought was the clincher. I wanted to see if Fred B. Allen would flinch. "Bob Fenster and Softex knew, and had dealings with the other six of The Seven. None of the other six knew *all* of the remaining six."

He shrugged, but he didn't flinch.

18

Wiggy and I were having lunch in the Softex cafeteria as the guest of President Kenny Irving in fact, but not in person. He had his peanuts. I was regaling Wiggy with my thoughts.

The cafeteria was light and airy with a wall of windows opposite a wall of food, which turned out to be rather good. Wiggy had said her interviews led her nowhere, but both women claimed to know Fred B. Allen—though, not well. We decided since he was the higher-up of the trio it might not be surprising that he didn't know them. Still, I thought that was worth looking into. After lunch we would trade personnel, I'd talk to the women, she to the boy.

I realized Fred B. Allen, computer-software whiz, could have been one of those psychotic guys who could say *any*thing and breeze through a lie-detector test. But I really had no basis to suspect him. On the other hand, Bob Fenster *was* killed by a guy who knew his routines.

Caloriewise, we were getting in the higher numbers. The deeper we got, the more paranoid I became. My principal had put another man on the job. He could upstage me. He could get there first. He is, after all, a hundred-dollar-an-hour man, so that ought to connote a professional.

After lunch I headed for Fred B. Allen's supervisor, Jim Forester. He was one of those guys you could picture jogging down the street dragging a tire behind him for the extra challenge.

"I'm satisfied with him most of the time," he said of Fred. "Seems devoted."

"Productive?"

"Yeah, sometimes." The supervisor gave me a look that seemed to question if I could be trusted with the truth. I returned him my trust-me gaze.

"Hard to gauge production in this game sometimes. With Fred, it often seems like he's on the verge of a great thing, then he just falls short. You know it doesn't quite come to fruition. But he seems devoted. Works long hours, hardly takes any time off—one, two days at the most—once, twice a year."

"Could you give me those dates?"

"Sure. I'll have personnel do you a print-out."

"Who hired him?"

"Fenster himself," he said. "He knew the application we were after."

"Developed it, didn't he?"

He nodded.

"Completed it here?"

"It was pretty well completed when he got here," he said.

"So, you didn't need him?"

"Oh, yes we did," he corrected me with a firmness born of deep conviction. "Lot of ins and outs needed looking after, fine tuning."

"And Allen supplied that?"

He frowned. "Yess," he drew out the sibilant in indecision, "in a manner of speaking…"

"What do you mean?"

"I'm not sure. It was almost as though he didn't want us to succeed with the application. Like it was his baby and he didn't want to part with it. Of course, he would have had no trouble justifying that to himself."

"How so?"

"You know the history. Program Arts went under after an unsuccessful challenge of our turf."

"I heard it the other way. They had the application;

you got the contract—ergo you had to produce the application and since Allen already produced it, you produced him, so to speak."

"All right, fair enough. That conveniently leaves out our existing dominance of the market, our licenses and customer bases, but it's too late in the game to quibble. Bob Fenster gave him a job—he didn't need to. We were close to breaking through on the application ourselves."

I didn't know how much of that was self-promotion, wish fulfillment, nor did I know how to determine it. "So why hire Allen?"

"Time—money—save on both," he said.

"But it didn't work."

"Not totally, no," he said. "We never were completely satisfied with Allen's efforts. As I said, it was as though he was always holding some vital component back."

"So why is he still here?"

"He's brilliant. We bring him along to the point he is about to submit a completed application, then we bring in a team of guys to overcome his phobia."

"Ever think he's out to sabotage the company?" I asked.

"It's crossed my mind," he said.

"Think he might have killed Bob Fenster?"

There was a long, noncommittal pause while his eyes seemed to turn to glass. "It's crossed my mind," he said.

Even with that incriminating pronouncement from Fred B. Allen's supervisor, I couldn't see him involved in a deed so foul. Then I realized it was difficult for me to visualize anyone blowing up his fellow man.

"How well do you know Fred Allen?"

He spread his hands— "Just an employee," he explained.

"Ever been to his house?"

He shook his head.

"He to yours?"

"No."

"Ever speak to anyone who knew him personally?"

"To Victor Nulty," he said, "for a reference when we hired him."

"What did he say about him?"

"Nothing but good. Called him a genius, as I remember."

"Is he a genius?"

"Who knows?" he said. "That word takes a beating. He's super-bright with developing—up to a point. Then he turns stupid. I don't think I'd call him a genius, no."

"Does he have any friends?"

"I doubt it. I've never seen him with anyone."

"You think you could get me his address?"

He frowned. "What for?"

"I'm trying to solve a crime," I reminded him. "And maybe prevent another."

"So, you'll go out there and ransack his house?"

"Not necessarily," I said. "Maybe just surprise him there. See how he reacts—turns red—keeps the door closed—tries to hide something."

He gave it some thought, then pushed a button on his phone and asked for the address. He wrote it on a piece of paper, then handed it to me.

"Oh—thanks," I said holding up my hand like a traffic cop. "Could you get me the days he took off—last three years?"

He relayed the message and waited while the information was retrieved from what I could only think of as a state-of-the-art system. Sure enough, in less than a minute we had our dates. I checked them quickly and was struck by what seemed like an odd coincidence.

Or was it?

The days Fred B. Allen took off coincided nicely with the dates of the bombings—with another few thrown in for preparations or to sidetrack an investigation.

Now all we had to do was make that odd coincidence more than a coincidence, and more than odd.

19

I knew it was a mistake to tell Wiggy about my plan. I couldn't shake her off the notion she should go along.

We pulled in front of the one-story house on Mulberry Street in a neighborhood of once-modest homes. Inflation in real estate and neighborhood cachet coupled with the pay scale at Softex had lifted the values beyond reach of the working stiffs who built the neighborhood. As a result, most of the properties were well taken care of. You could tell an upwardly-mobile from an original owner by the length of the grass in the front lawn and the era of the paint on the house.

Many of the houses were redecorated to relieve the monotony of stucco. Fred B. Allen's house was stucco, but it looked like it had been applied with a shovel. Next door was a New England saltbox sheathed in cedar shingles. Down the street a Palladian villa—all had their origins in a thirteen-hundred-square-foot stucco shoe box.

The thing we noticed right away about Fred's house was the second story on the detached garage. It stood like a lookout over the neighborhood.

"Let's not park in front," Wiggy said, and I pulled the car two doors down. I didn't want to get too far away in case we were called upon to make a hasty exit from the premises.

The neighborhood was called Willow Glen and was old enough to sport many mature trees. Fred B. Allen's house seemed to be in some kind of forest, with towering pines, sycamores and liquidambars. There was even a *Washingtonia filifera* in the backyard.

I tried to suggest for sanity's sake Wiggy stay in the car. She would have none of it.

"Two people have twice the chance of being spotted," I said.

"But a man and a woman together look less suspicious."

We made our way to the front path.

"Be nice if some friendly housekeeper answers the door and offers to give us a tour," I said. But that was not to be. No one answered our knock. Wiggy tried the door.

"You didn't expect it to be unlocked?" I said.

"You never know," she said.

A gentle whirring sound drew our eyes to the faux light fixture over the door, which was telescoping toward us in the form of a video camera. Instinctively, we hid our faces with our hands and turned to scurry around the side of the house via the driveway to the garage.

"Nice gimmick," I said.

"You think he went to all that trouble to keep the religious proselytizers at bay?"

"Not too likely, is it?"

We tried to peer in the windows, but they were all efficiently blocked with shades and curtains.

At the back door, we were ready for the hidden camera when it made its appearance. We ducked around the corner on the garage side of the house.

"You think those things take any pictures?" I asked. "Or are they just for intimidation?"

"With a computer nerd, you never know," Wiggy said.

"So now what?" I asked rather rhetorically.

"We get in."

I chuckled the chuckle of the fearful. "On camera," I said.

We then toured the perimeter of the house while

Wiggy tried all the windows—also locked.

Together our eyes drifted upward.

"Santa Claus," Wiggy said.

"What?"

"Down the chimney."

I looked at our physiques. Since I was carrying roughly twice the weight she was, I suggested that if anyone would fit down a chimney it would be she.

She said, "Nonsense, Santa Claus is much fatter than you are."

"Thanks," I said.

She giggled—"I don't care *who* you are, fatso, get your reindeer off my roof!"

"Very funny," I said, "but we're no closer to pay ground."

"Pay ground?" she asked.

"It means our goal," I explained patiently.

"Pay dirt," she corrected me. People loved to correct me. She looked at the garage, then the second story. "Workroom," she said.

"What?"

"Looks like a workroom up there."

"How can you tell from down here?"

"What else? If you wanted to make bombs, where would you do it, in the bathtub?"

I looked up—Then I climbed the stairs. Wiggy stayed put on the driveway. The door was locked. I turned from the camera I expected, but didn't see, and looked over the roof of the house. There I saw several skylights.

Back on terra solid, I conferred with Wiggy. She handed me her Swiss Army knife. "I never leave home without it," she said. "It has a screwdriver gizmo—maybe you can pry open a skylight."

I climbed a sycamore tree whose spreading branches took me close enough to jump to the roof.

The skylights were clear glass and I could see into most rooms of a crammed and disheveled abode. Books, magazines, newspapers, cardboard boxes everywhere. I thought I was staring into the face of genius as I moved from skylight to skylight. Troubled genius. The junk he had all over the place made me think he had more things in common with Victor Nulty than Program Arts.

I didn't see any signs of a bomb-making facility, but I didn't know what that should look like. If making bombs was as easy as they said, you didn't need any special paraphernalia.

Before breaking into the house, which looked like nothing more than a recluse hovel, I went back up the tree and made a jump to the garage roof. There were two more skylights. I was pleased Fred B. Allen fancied skylights, but these were obscure glass with a band of copper holding them in place.

I took out Wiggy's Swiss Army knife and went to work. I got so wrapped up in my task that I didn't realize Wiggy was climbing the tree and joining me until I heard the thud on the roof and felt like my heart was shooting out of my throat.

I scolded her. "You scared the lights out of me! You should stay down there in case we need to go for the police...or an ambulance..."

"The police? You're kidding. We should get them up here to watch us breaking and entering?"

"If we find something..." I said lamely.

"What?" She was talking sense for a change.

"Incriminating stuff," I said vaguely. "I don't know what. But if we don't look, we certainly won't find anything."

I had gotten the copper edging loose enough to slide the glass out sufficiently for me to drop into the room. I wanted Wiggy to stay up there, but naturally she would have none of it.

The roof was not very high from the floor, and holding the edge of the skylight support, I easily lowered myself into the room. The first thing I noticed was the huge TV screen on the wall. It must have been six foot by six foot. Then I saw the elaborate computer setup, and then I saw

Wiggy lowering herself to wrap her legs on my shoulders.

We landed a few feet from a computer-console setup that had the potential for making Bob Fenster envious. Reluctantly, I disengaged Wiggy. I didn't know much about computers myself, but I could see Wiggy was enthralled. Before I knew it, she was pushing buttons.

"Look at this!" she said, as the menu came up on the huge screen. But then we were interrupted by Big Brother.

The screen on the north wall lit up with a larger-than-life-sized moving picture of Fred B. Allen. He was dressed in the coat and tie we had seen him in at Softex, and his expression carried the weight of an overworked funeral director.

"Hello," he said from the screen, his mouth moving in perfect sync with the words, like a flight attendant telling you to fasten your seat belt. "You have entered my private property without my permission." He shook his head, clucked his tongue and let us know how distressed he felt at the news—as some sadistic teacher might feel catching an errant pupil in a punishable offense.

"I don't have to tell you breaking into someone else's property is a criminal offense," he said from the screen, his delivery notably devoid of compassion, or even a dollop of human warmth. "I could, of course, have the police called automatically and trap you in place until they come. But I have a better idea. Make yourself comfortable, for in five seconds you will hear a beep that will indicate the motion sensors are activated. When that happens, I will give you further instructions." He paused.

"Let's get out of here," I said, and heard the beep sound, like a microwave oven signaling the stuff is cooked.

Like we were.

Big Brother was spouting off again: "There—the motion sensors are activated. Now if you move outside of the three-foot radius around where you are now, I regret to tell you, you will set off detonation of several bombs which will quite suddenly extinguish your life. A bit harsh, you say? But then breaking into private property *is* against the law."

Wiggy and I looked at each other, our eyes bulging with fear.

But, we didn't move.

20

We were both drenched in perspiration and too scared to talk. Wiggy broke the stillness and her soft voice was like shattering glass. "Singular," she said.

"Huh?" I whispered.

"He spoke in the singular. Like there was only one of us..."

"Yeah—so what? It's a motion-activated recording," I said. "Can't tell if there's one or a hundred. Good bet it's only one, though."

"Bad bet this time."

"Maybe."

"Yeah, maybe because there are two of us, we can bring something off he didn't foresee."

"Yeah, like what?"

"I don't know."

"It only takes one move to set off the bomb and I guess we don't doubt he has the expertise to bring it off."

"No, we don't doubt it."

"So, either of us move, we both blow up."

She looked up to the skylight. "Maybe we can get out like we came. Maybe he didn't think to wire the skylight," she said, hopefully. "Didn't see any wires or anything, did you?"

I made a quick assessment of the place. The entry door was on the east wall, straight across from this computer setup on the west wall. There was a window beside the console—and a window on the south wall overlooking the house. I didn't see anything that looked like motion sensors, but then, I didn't know what motion sensors looked like.

We seemed to be about five feet from the floor area under the skylight—over three feet by the most optimistic estimate.

It didn't look like we were going anywhere.

"I don't see anything," I said, "but, I'm not willing to doubt him."

Wiggy turned back to the computer buttons and the quaintly named "mouse" that roved at her prodding back and forth on the table.

"Hey!" I was shocked to see her blithely ignore the warning. "What are you doing?"

"I'm going back to the menu."

"But...the bomb."

"Hey, he said three feet. I'm here. It's no three feet. Besides, I've already moved the mouse and nothing's happened."

She was a lot more optimistic than I was. Intriguing categories came upon the monitor screen in front of us. Fred B. Allen was a man with strong beliefs in good and evil. We had:

Lust
Pornography
Monopoly
Militia
Conspiracies

and more, but Wiggy wisely stopped the mouse at conspiracies and clicked into a sub-menu and another list:

AIDS
JFK
7

Another click on 7: and there they were.

Bob Fenster
Philip Carlisle
Winston Chambers
Gideon Golan

Harold Mattlock
Ludwig Duesberg
Frank B. Smithson

"Not alphabetical," Wiggy noted.

"No—listed in order of demise. Mattlock is next."

"You think Fred could go after the rest of them while we're frozen in our three feet?"

"He could do maybe one more before we starve to death or blow up, whichever occurs first," I said.

"Mattlock," she murmured.

"Bring up Bob Fenster," I said.

She did. The entry started with his biography—obviously written by Fred B. Allen, beginning with a reasonable enough tone then slinking into darker slime.

> ...not satisfied with unprecedented success in market share and product dominance, Bob Fenster developed an overpowering ego, with a just-folks persona. And no one stood in his way long. No one dared compete in any field remotely connected to anything Fenster had touched or might want to control. Control was the key to his persona. Bob Fenster wanted to control the world. Not only through software and his company, Softex, but the daily operation of every facet of our existence. He must be stopped.

Wiggy and I shared a soft sigh. "Let's see what he says about Mattlock," I said. She moved the mouse until Mattlock came up along with his picture. Allen had apparently refined his methods, for now instead of reading the bio in cold type we were treated to an audio narration by our host himself.

> Harold Mattlock, of foreign birth,
> took our country lock, stock and bar-

rel with his media empire. Mattlock has a genius for manipulating politicians to the everlasting enrichment of his purse. One of the leading enrichers of Mattlock's purse has been Bob Fenster with egomaniacal advertisements featuring pictures of his simple person casually dressed belying his sinister megalomania. For this collusion and enrichment by an immoral man, he must be stopped.

And so it was, down through the list, with each justification for murder ending with "he must be stopped." We fanned through the entire file. It was obvious Mattlock's number was up, though when was not immediately apparent.

Then by chance we saw an item:

Timetable

The mouse did its duty—

There were the dates of all the bombings, and the scheduled dates for the next three. Mattlock's was tomorrow.

While I was absorbing the blow, Wiggy was surfing with the mouse. We almost forgot our three-foot restrictions, so absorbed were we in the fare from the screen. Wiggy seemed to be taking a step back, so I grabbed her and we both had a heart-stopping moment.

The screen flipped at Wiggy's beck and call to pornography. A respectable or disrespectable subject, I suppose, depending on your viewpoint. Fred's was strongly anti. There was a series of pictures that must have been pornographic before someone (presumably Fred) had blanked out the intimate details. Then a written diatribe against the evils of the flesh. It was as though Fred couldn't trust his voice to the exposé of harsh judgments.

"Pervert," Wiggy said. "I think he's some kind of pervert," she said.

"Prude maybe," I said.

"Yeah, but look at this stuff," Wiggy argued. "He's weirder than a prude. A prude wouldn't put all these pictures in the system. A prude wouldn't want to *look* at them. There is something real weird going on in this sleazeball's head."

Some time passed while we were both plunged deep in thought. Survival thoughts.

"Well," Wiggy said at last, "at least we know one thing."

"What?"

"We found our man."

"Hm, yeah, well, maybe," I said. "But what proof do we have?"

"Proof? This isn't proof enough?"

"What? That we broke into his place and he threatens via some computer gimmick to blow us up? Even if we don't blow up, what is our evidence he's it? Our suspicion?"

"Well, but what about that stuff on the computer?"

I shrugged. "Even if he doesn't destroy it and doesn't destroy us, it really is circumstantial. A lot of the guys in the Hermosa Beach group could have that stuff on their computers. I wouldn't be surprised if it was a program he sends out."

"No way," Wiggy was not in accord.

We sank again into silence.

"A quarter for your thoughts," I said.

"That one goes a *penny* for your thoughts."

"Inflation," I said.

"I was just thinking, if he blows us up, we'll have our proof. Only we won't be around to do anything about it."

"Hm—but where's the logic here?" I asked. "He's going to blow us up and risk what the ensuing investigation will uncover? I mean is the risk worth it to him?"

"Well, this computer stuff would go with us," she said. "Think he's just playing with us?"

"Could be—" I said hopefully. "Could very well be."

"He's doing a good job of it," she said.

"We better decide our options."

"How many are there? We try to get out through the skylight—the motion sensors go off or they don't."

"Ditto the door," I said, and we both looked at the door with a simple dead bolt we could turn and make a clean break. The room itself was less cluttered than the house. I wondered aloud—"What about the house? Do you think if we'd gone in there we would have gotten the same treatment?"

"The TV screen and all?" she asked. "I don't know. You?"

"Must," I said.

"But would he really blow up his house?"

"If someone was on to him, why not?" I said. "He probably rents."

"Think he's thought this all through?" she asked.

"I'd have a hard time believing he didn't," I said. "He is one thorough piece of work, this guy."

"Yeah," she said, looking over the room. "I don't see the slightest evidence of any sensors or wires or anything, do you?"

Except for the giant screen and the computer setup, the room looked like you would imagine a room over a garage to look. A room that had been left unfinished, with studs showing.

We were saved further speculation by the sound of a car screeching to a sudden stop in the driveway.

Wiggy and I looked at each other. "What's our plan?" she asked.

"We don't have one," I had to admit. "If he comes busting in here I guess we don't have to worry about motion sensors."

"I think it's a bluff," she said.

"So do I." I heard footsteps.

"Do you want to chance it?"

Before I could answer in the negative, the door burst open and we were looking at Fred B. Allen, his eyebrows a jingle, his eyes beady and deranged. His plain necktie was rising and falling with his exercised breath, like climbing the flight of stairs had overcome his equilibrium.

So much for motion sensors. He didn't need them. We were looking down the barrel of a pretty hefty firearm.

21

His eyes were set even closer to one another than I remembered; making it easier for one eye to keep an eye on the other. Not a bad idea for a man of his character. I suppose I should have been relieved Wiggy wasn't the culprit, but my mind for the nonce was elsewhere.

"Start talking," he said.

"I'm speechless," I said.

"Criminal offense," he said. "Breaking and entering."

I nodded.

"So, what are you doing here?"

"We were just passing by and we fell in the roof through the skylight. We would have happily left long ago, but this guy came on the TV and told us we'd blow up if we moved."

"So, we stayed," Wiggy said, giving Fred B. the sultry eye.

"So, what are your plans?" he asked.

"Depends," I said. "If we don't take a bullet, you mean?"

"Yeah."

"Thanks for asking," I said. "Our immediate plans would be to get as far from here as soon as possible."

He nodded, but I couldn't tell if it was a nod of approbation or one of skepticism.

"And the police?"

"If you want to have us arrested, it's okay by me," I said. "Call 'em. I'll plead guilty."

He seemed to be considering that, but I didn't know if he was wondering if I were that stupid, or if I thought *he* were that stupid.

"I'd rather call the undertaker and get it over with," he said.

I didn't like the sound of that.

"Why kill us?" Wiggy asked with a guileless innocence that warmed my heart.

"Why not?"

"The electric chair, maybe," she said. "Not a nice way to go."

Between us, without discussing it, Wiggy and I seemed to have decided to play it pretty dumb. We really had found nothing directly incriminating.

"So what are you doing here?" he asked. As if he didn't know.

"Look," I said. "We're investigating the seven murders. We've talked to a lot of people. This home visit is just part of the process. I did the same to your old boss."

"He doesn't have the guts..."

"Yes, and neither do you apparently."

Fred B. Allen tensed on the trigger. His whole frame went rigid. "What's that supposed to mean?" he demanded.

I shrugged my shoulders as nonchalantly as I could. "We didn't find anything here either."

Those close-set eyes seemed to get closer.

"Of course, if anyone gets shot here, it could cause some suspicion," I said, playing to him. "Might trigger a close investigation"—I was chagrined at my choice of the word "trigger" but it was already out of the barrel, so to speak.

I wish I could say I had softened him in some way, but I saw only hardening.

The sun was slipping down through the west window and starting to shine on his hairline. Soon it would be in his eyes. It gave me an exciting moment of hope which in short order I dashed. Even if he were blindfolded, he had the gun, and if he was at the door, he could have shot a roomful of intruders, even though he couldn't see them. If only I had a gun...then I thought of the Swiss Army knife—would I dare try? I had no experience throwing knives. Most likely I'd miss and then be shot—in self-defense.

But suppose I threw and hit the target? Then we found he was not the serial killer, just a guy protecting his home from intruders. Now we are guilty of murder and breaking and entering and it would not take a very clever district attorney to make a case for the death penalty.

"Okay," I said, "Mr. Allen—why don't you put the gun down—we'll leave, we'll talk, we'll do whatever you want."

"You're scum," he snarled.

"In that case," I said, "we're hardly worth shooting."

He was skeptical. "What good are you?"

"What good would we be to you if we were dead?"

"Getting too damned nosy."

"Well, yeah, that's my job," I said, but added hastily, "but we didn't find anything."

"Didn't have much time to look," he mumbled.

"Mean we'd find something if we did?"

"Maybe."

"What?"

"That's for me to know," he said.

A sudden thought occurred to me. If the motion sensors were a fiction, maybe the gun he was holding was empty. If he were not the bomber, there would certainly be no sense in killing us. On the different hand, if he were the bomber and made us Swiss cheese with that cannon he was sporting, we could probably be sure he was the killer. But being dead, we couldn't do much with that knowledge.

"So, who do you think is blowing these people up?" I asked out of the pink.

"I've no idea."

"Come on, you must know something. Fenster was

the target—all the others were tied to him. One of the club did it—or had it done if he wasn't skilled enough."

"You're entitled to your opinion."

"What's your opinion?" Wiggy asked him.

He jerked his head as though he had been suddenly frightened. "I don't know what you are talking about!"

"No? Then why are you pointing that gun at us?" I asked him. "Lot of people break in here?"

"You never know," he said.

I looked around the room. "You know, I don't see anything worth hiding. Where do you make the bombs?"

"I don't make any bombs."

"Then why are you still sticking that gun in our faces?"

"Because you're criminals, trying to rip me off."

"Well, you caught us now. Call the police—have us arrested, then take an inventory. See if we've taken anything." I was trying everything I could think of.

"You don't seem to me to be in any position to tell me what to do."

"Touché," I said, and knew right away I was being too flip. Fred B. Allen tensed on the trigger again and changed his coloring to a hue that smacked of jaundiced liver. He sure was a nervous Nancy with that firearm. "So what do *you* want to do, shoot us?"

"I'm thinking about it."

"So, what is holding you back? The electric chair?"

He snorted as though that were insignificant.

"Yeah, I guess that's pretty stupid. What's a couple more corpses? If you don't get the chair for blowing up those heavy-hitters, who's going to get worked up about a couple nobodies?"

"Precisely," he said, licking his lips. Was that, I wondered, an admission? Some inner voice told me it was time to tread lightly.

"Why don't you let Wiggy go? We'll talk it over man-to-man. You want to shoot me when we're finished, okay. But I don't peg you for a guy who goes around killing women—all The Seven are men."

"Let her go? Are you crazy? To the police?"

"Why not?—as you pointed out, we're the criminals here. What have you got to lose?"

"Yeah," he said, like he didn't agree.

"Fenster had it coming," I blurted out. Fred B. Allen jerked his head in a gratifying reaction. I rolled with it. "When you get that rich, you've got to get more considerate of others. *Noblesse oblige*. I mean here he is the richest guy in the world and he's still fighting tooth and screw to bury the competition. A little competition wouldn't hurt him."

"Little?" Fred said, "we were more than a little. We made real inroads—we could have gone toe-to-toe with him."

"And so you should have. Any other guy would have seen your program was superior and the country would be better off for having the two of you in the marketplace."

"Right."

"But Fenster couldn't let go, could he?"

"No."

"So somebody had to get rid of him. It was inevitable. All of history is the story of closing the gap between the rich and the poor—and it's always a struggle. In twelfth century England, they killed all the people with smooth hands. That must have been pretty effective. Now we have the income tax. That's not so effective—so, I think you did the right thing." Wiggy was shaking her head at my babble.

Fred was watching me. His attention was rapt. The sun was working on his forehead. He didn't seem aware of it. I wondered why he didn't just move out of the way, then I thought it might have been his concentration on what I was saying, so I kept at it.

"And the funny thing is, I can even sympathize with the other hits. They were all of a piece, weren't they?"

The close-set eyes were still on me, drilling in without giving me much clue to what went on behind them.

"They all conspired to ruin your dreams.

Government is supposed to keep the playing fields even, not tilt them to the super-rich. *They* don't need any help. Why is it the worthy guys who need so much help so often get dumped on by the big boys? It's not only unfair, it's stupid. They don't know their history—or they're too naive to think it couldn't happen again—a mass slaughter of the smooth hands."

Did he steal a glance at his hands? I wasn't sure.

Suddenly the sun hit him in the eyes. "Let's separate," I whispered into Wiggy's ear. "Go to the screen." By the time Fred had moved we were on opposite sides of the room. No bomb went off. So much for the motion-sensor myth. In the split-second interval, I had put my hand in my pocket to feel the cold comfort of the Swiss Army knife.

"Hey," Fred said, "get your hand out of your pocket."

I shook my head, I was trembling.

"What's in there?"

"I've got you covered, Fred. You can shoot me, but my reflexes will pull this trigger and that'll be the end of you."

He looked over at Wiggy, then back at me. He obviously didn't like us separated. "Get back together," he commanded, waving the gun.

I shook my head again. He kept turning the gun and his body from one to the other of us. He looked like a man adrift, control slipping away.

Then Wiggy astonished us both. She began taking off her clothes.

22

"Hey! What are you doing?" Fred B. Allen demanded. But instead of looking lascivious, he looked shocked and
frightened. *Was* he a prude? I don't know what Wiggy
intended, but she *was* unsettling him.

I couldn't blame him. She undressed with such
grace, such gentleness. Even I, who had been privy to
Wiggy's particular charms, couldn't take my eyes off her.
Poor Fred! How long had it been since he had seen a glis-
tening, perfect body like Wiggy's? Probably never. And from
the look of his agitation, he may well never have seen any
woman without her clothes on.

And it was not just the picture-perfect form that ani-
mated him, it was the whole vision of loveliness she project-
ed as her arms raised to the roof and seemed just incidentally
to take her sweater with them. That tangle of natural-knit
goods floated to a pile on the floor like an owl with all its
vested intelligence settling in for the day. The skirt dropped
like water off the trunk of a queen palm, quickly, cleanly,
leaving the trunk shimmering in its purity.

I thought Fred's eyes were going to fall out of his
head. He waved the gun. "Stop!" he shouted. "No more!"

But Wiggy paid him no heed. The bra and panties
were lacy black, and couldn't have been better selected for
the occasion. When you think how often a woman must take
off a brassiere, it should not be surprising that the maneuver
is executed with some skill. Wiggy's was consummate,

though it is a rather unnatural contortion of arms and hands. The creator of the female body could not have considered the eventual employment of such a contraption. But Wiggy made removing it seem effortless and artful, revealing the blessings of nature.

"Hey, cut it out!" Fred's protests were getting weaker, his perspiration stronger. He pinched his eyes suddenly closed, and just as my fingers tightened on the Swiss Army knife, he just as suddenly opened them.

Wiggy's fingers were in the waistband of the remaining black lace.

"STOP IT!" Fred yelled. He pointed the gun at me, as though he wanted me to make her stop.

"Hey, Wiggy," I said, without much spirit. "Fred doesn't like you undressing here." And it came out like the most normal conversation, putting Fred out of joint even more. The gun wavered in its focus, sometimes in sync with Fred, sometimes not. I didn't know a lot about guns, but I did know if he was planning to shoot it, he would need more control and at least a modicum of focus.

But Wiggy was not to be dissuaded. Those tantalizing fingers in her panty's waistband worked their way toward the floor, where she stepped out of the hip-hugging black lace with, I thought, more seductive movements than heretofore. When she stood across the room from him just as she had come into the world, she pursed her lips in a kiss. Well, she wasn't exactly as she came into the world, she had grown quite a bit and filled out in a lot of delightful locations.

We were like three statues, frozen in time and that time just laid there, begging one of us to move.

My mind was whirling and getting nowhere. Obviously, Wiggy had latched onto his prudery or perversion and was trying to put him off his barley—but to what avail? He still had the gun and I was not about to play cowboys and Native Americans. In my relatively short career as a P.I., I have never developed an immunity to bullets.

"Hey—yoh," I heard Wiggy say. "Aren't one of you

guys going to undress?"

Fred looked at me with a jerk of his head, the pistol still pointed at Wiggy. "Put your clothes back on!" he barked.

"Hey, what's a matter, honey," she cooed. "You're not afraid of girls, are you?" She took a step toward him. He gasped. Then another step.

"Hey! Stop that."

She took another. I estimated three more would put her on target.

Fred raised the gun to her nose level. "Another step and you're dead meat."

She pursed her lips and shook her head as though he were disappointing her. "You don't want to do that, honey," she said. "I'm much better live meat," and she gave him one of those sultry Marilyn Monroe looks. He cringed. She took a half step—he steadied the pistol.

"That was only a half step, honey," she said. "Why don't you come to me? Let's make love, not war."

Another half step and they were close enough to reach out their arms and touch fingertips—Wiggy tried it— her long, slender arms floating toward her adversary like she was a one-woman United Nations.

But Fred B. Allen was a nation adverse to the kind of aid she was offering. He was shuddering now like a chill had overtaken his susceptible, frail body. What went through his mind? Could Wiggy tell? It was fairly obvious he wasn't happy with her seduction, but maybe that was because I was there to add the disapproving element. Would it have been different if it were just the two of them?

"Fred," I said gently, "would you like me to leave?— I can wait outside…"

He shipped the gun around and pointed it where I had little trouble seeing it. "You stay where you are," he commanded. I obeyed.

So, why wasn't he shooting? So far it had all been empty threats. The phony motion sensors, the waving gun. Obviously he had doubts. But just as obviously, I wasn't eager to make a wrong move that might provoke him to shoot. And I wondered if Wiggy wasn't pushing Fred critically close to the point of explosion. She was so close to him now, if she took another step, his options would be to embrace her, back away from her, or shoot her.

It wasn't a lot of options. My hand was still fiddling with the Swiss Army knife in my pocket, but I was having no luck trying to open it with one hand. Yet I wondered what I would do if I got it open—lunge at him? That would be enough to set the most pacific man with a gun in his hand to fire in self-defense. I didn't want to give him that option. Yet, I wanted to have the option of having a weapon should that prove useful.

They seemed to be at a standoff—naked Wiggy and shivering Fred.

Wiggy reached out to Fred again. "Go on," she purred, "touch me." Fred recoiled and pointed the trembling pistol at her navel, as though that would be a good place to shoot because there was already an indentation there and it would be harder to detect a bullet hole.

"What's a matter, sweetie?" she taunted him again. "Don't you like girls?"

He licked his lips in a manner that said he liked them all too well.

"Take off your clothes, sweetie."

"No!"

"Why not?"

"Filthy."

"Rather look at boys?"

"Don't be ridiculous!"

"Come on," she said, taking tiny, slow steps toward him, "don't be afraid. Show me what you are made of."

I was shaking in my shoes. She was acting crazy—just giving that crazy Fred enough encouragement to shoot us both.

Then I took my eyes off Wiggy de Milo and saw Fred was in worse shape than I was. Was that froth at the corner of his mouth?

"Come on then—touch me," she said, and held out her arms.

"*Don't touch me!*" he shouted.

She frowned. "Why not?"

"You're not clean."

"Well, yes I am too," she said.

"Slut!"

"Now, that's not very nice," Wiggy said. "I'm offering you the purest feeling two people can share and you call me names. Why do you do that?"

"Harlot!"

"There's another one," she said. "Kind of old fashioned, but effective. You've missed a few," she said, then studying his reactions reeled off those he had missed, some going back to Shakespeare, some not.

His breathing was so labored by now, I thought he needed an oxygen mask.

"Is it...your...mother?" Wiggy asked, and Fred stiffened like rigor mortis had just taken him.

"Slut..." he murmured.

"Tell me about it," Wiggy pleaded softly.

"Slut, *Slut*, SLUT!"

"Your mother was..."

The shot rang out as though it had been fired in a garbage can, pinging and resonating with metallic reverberation that put me in mind of a shooting gallery at a low-rent carnival.

It happened so fast I'm not sure how it happened, but Wiggy went down oozing blood—so profusely I almost fainted.

"Hello"—the big screen was talking to us—to the three of us. Big Brother, Fred B. Allen, was talking to himself. "You have entered my private property without my permission..."

Fred raised the pistol and fired at the big screen, stopping himself in mid-sentence. Then, he turned toward the computer console and shot out the screen, and fired at the hard drive. Bullets were ringing out and I was counting, but I had no idea how many the thing in Fred's hand held.

Then like a morose robot, Fred moved the gun to his head. Unaccountably, I rushed him and tackled him, knocking him to the floor, as the gun clicked, the dry, mocking sound of an empty chamber. He was out of bullets.

I swung my attention to Wiggy on the floor beside us. She had reclaimed her underpants and was staunching a wound in her upper thigh with them.

Fred B. Allen was making the breathy sounds of emotional exhaustion, preparatory to complete collapse.

"Good work, Gil," Wiggy said and I never felt such an uplift from a compliment.

Fred B. Allen was offering little resistance by this time. He had virtually subdued himself. I was in command. He was the real wimp.

Real men don't mail bombs that kill people.

23

I finally got that Swiss Army knife open as I was sitting on Fred's back with the blade loosely held at the back of his neck. The option was for Wiggy to sit her naked body on him, but Fred quickly opted for me instead, while she threw on her duds and went next door to call the cops.

The local constabulary was both friendly and efficient and cheerfully took over custody of Fred B. Allen who had by this time wimped himself to a frazzle.

And fortunately for us, he had not destroyed all his disc memory in the shoot up, and the jury of his peers would later find sufficient evidence to ship him to the slammer in perpetuity.

The news was greeted by Harold Mattlock with a huge sigh of relief.

"As soon as I verify the pertinent facts, I'll have the money wired to your account," he said graciously. "Let's see, that was one million, right?"

I hope he didn't hear me gulp when I said, "Right."

"You'll have it tomorrow at the latest," he said.

"Thank you, sir."

"And, Gil..."

"Yes, sir?"

"Thank *you*."

Harold Mattlock was certainly the best guy I worked for to date. He was living proof that to be rich you didn't have to be a schlemiel.

His thanks, so sincere, so heartfelt, were almost more important to me than the money.

Almost. But now, thanks to that fee, I netted enough to buy that house next door to expand my palm garden—and rent it out, putting me on the road to being a real-estate mogul just like Daddybucks Wemple. Or, in the alternative, I could tell my control-freak of a father-in-law to take a flying leap over Niagara Falls in a barrel of cement, all expenses paid by his *nouveau riche* son-in-law.

Appealing as the former alternative was, I decided on the latter and spent a good deal of time rehearsing my presentation.

"You sack of dandruff," I'd begin, "I'm blowing this joint. You're nothing but a cheapskate who is so tight he squeaks when he walks—which from the look of your gut is not nearly often enough."

A local sawbones patched Wiggy up in a jiffy. Apparently, Fred B. Allen hadn't the heart to hurt her because he certainly had the means. But then he probably didn't think she was one of the unlucky seven he saw as the ultimate threat to mankind. But that seven business was a ruse. All seven led to Bob Fenster and Softex, and Fred had gotten more than halfway through his murderous scheme.

"Geez, Wiggy," I said, when we left the doc who assured us she would be okay in no time, "you took an awful chance—"

"Yeah," she said. "How would you disarm a mad bomber?"

"Not by taking off my clothes, that's for sure."

I flew back home with Wiggy who pronounced, "Well, I guess it's back to your wife with you." I started to argue, but she put her hand over my mouth.

I told her her cut would be forthcoming and she resisted taking it. But when I let her in on the story, she couldn't believe it.

But Wiggy didn't need money, she protested. "The boob-and-bun bobber took good care of me," she said referring to her ex—the plastic surgeon.

"No, no," I insisted. "Buy some cycads with it," I said.

"Sike what? Heads?"

"A rare plant," I said. "Just a thought."

"I'll give that some serious thought," she said unseriously.

When we landed in L.A., I offered to see her home. She declined. "I don't want to do anything that might pop my stitches," she said.

"I won't, I promise."

She smiled and shook her head. "But I'd *want* to," she said. She kissed me on the cheek at the curb. She wouldn't even let me share the cab. "Call me for lunch sometime," she said, and I choked back a surfeit of tears.

"Oh, and Gil—"

"Yeah?"

"You write the book—"

"No, I promised..."

"No, no, it's okay, really. I *want* you to."

"Well..."

"Really—"

"If I ever do, I'd share the royalties."

"Not necessary." She was in the cab and waving good-bye when I said, "I insist." But she was already down the street.

I took the van to save ten dollars—and we circled the airport twice before we filled up.

The house was empty when I got there. I had forgotten Tyranny Rex had booked another sale for her glass menagerie. I'd have another couple days of peace.

I went like a bumblebee flying a direct route to my palms and cycads, and gloried in the modest new growth of both. An opening leaf on a *Syagrus oleracea* here, some new leaves fighting for life on an *Encephalartos friderici-guilielmi* which hadn't thrown any leaves since I got it two and a half years before.

I sized up the house next door. The for-sale sign was still up. Not much had ever been done to the landscape—

some dead grass and a few hardy, but marginal shrubs. I could turn it into a tropical paradise with my fee. Then, if I got another fee, I could keep going down the block making tropical paradises right here in Torrance, California.

But, I had made up my mind. My independence from the giant thumb of my father-in-law was more important than another measly quarter acre to expand my palms. There could be no substitute for the exhilaration I would feel telling Daddy Pimple where to go.

In the garage, my Plymouth chugged and coughed until my artful feet on the pedals, coordinated with magic hand on the key, kicked it into action. The Plymouth was my company car, supplied by Daddy Pimple after a nationwide search to find the world's cheapest deal.

Tomorrow I would shop for a Mercedes.

I rehearsed in my mind the definitive farewell address I would make Old Cheapo. I knew he would counter that the secretary had done my job in her lunch hour and done it better than I did, hands-down.

No matter. I'd tell him what a cheapskate he was— negligible raises in twenty-five years—niggardly policy for sick leave—and how sick of him I'd become! Mr. Dandruff, sometimes washing your hair helps that affliction!

You're so cheap you don't cool the water for the troops, just for the general. Well, I'll have all the cool water I want from now on.

The troops on the floor inside the Elbert A. Wemple and Associates, Realtors' airplane hangar of an office were listless as ever, befitting their regard for their boss.

Elbert A. Wemple, posturing pimple, was seated on his elevated platform, in his glass cage befitting an agile chimpanzee. Indeed it was difficult to imagine Daddy Pimple anywhere else. Moss was growing on his north side.

It was a heavy dandruff day and his ubiquitous brown suit was white from the shoulders down.

As soon as I stepped to the platform that served to set Daddybucks above the rest of us (indeed the only thing besides his obscene wealth that could do so), I fell into my old habit of cadging some of his exclusive chilled water.

"Malvin!" he blasted me. "Where the hell have you been?" he demanded, as though we hadn't gone all over it so painfully before. "It's been a real ball of snakes around here. Every damn pipe decided to break at once over on Artesia and the tenants are fit to be tied. Geezus, we needed the whole United States Navy to evacuate the place."

"Daddy Wemple," I said using my wife's beloved appellation for her father, "I've got to tell you something."

"No, you don't," he snapped. "I'm doing the talking here. We damn near had a tenant revolt over on Yukon. Damn electricity went off and we had the entire Edison Company out there looking for it—including old Tom Edison himself. Geezus—two days, no electricity—food ruined, no showers. I tell you it's been a real ball of snakes."

"That's too bad. I've got to tell you..."

"Damn it," his meaty hand made sudden and violent contact with his desk—"don't just stand there like a nincompoop, start putting out fires."

"But, I..."

"Oh, yeah," he wouldn't let me get a word in on its side. "That fruitcake you hired in Hermosa wants to rent to a family of hyenas. Take care of it."

I opened my mouth and nothing came out. I retreated, dumb, to my desk. I surrendered to the ugly, hard chair and thought again about the house next door. Maybe I could get a string of them first, *then* leave Daddybucks to suffocate in a pile of dandruff.

Besides, it's nice to feel needed.

Excerpts from *The Missing Link*
A Gil Yates Private Investigator Novel
By Alistair Boyle

He certainly was fond of talking. More than I am fond of listening. And of all places to experience logorrhea, a meeting of palm nuts should rightfully be near the bottom. There is zero communication with palm trees. Oh, a lot of people talk to them, but there is no documentary proof that any of them have ever talked back.

My new buddy is a gardener for one of the super-rich. Mr. Rich's got a whale of a palm collection, so Jack Kimback is here to bone up.

Now Jack gets to the meat of the thing. His boss, who is just too famous, in an illicit sort of way, to mention, is looking for a private detective to find his daughter.

He has interviewed every known agency, tried a few, and doesn't like any of them. He is apparently a very picky man, as can be seen in his hiring this erudite, well-spoken young man to tend his palms.

Said Megabucks has also had it with the cops and the missing persons folks. A man that rich, his gardener says, is used to buying what he wants, but his money, this time, isn't cutting the ketchup.

If you have ever felt possessed by the devil, you know how I felt when I heard the following words come out of my mouth:

"Oh, I just happen to *be* a private detective."

Jack's eyebrows hit the ceiling. You could tell he was skeptical that a mealy-mouthed guy like me would be in such a macho line of work.

It seemed like a harmless tease at first. I didn't look on it as a lie, exactly. A lark. I thought it would go no further. Any time now, I would set him straight–tell him I was only joking. But the more he told me, the more intrigued I became, and the less impetus I had for telling the technical truth.

You know what the "technical truth" is. It is something that only serves the science of mathematics. Every other human endeavor is necessarily fraught with nuances, with shadings, with spared feelings, with personal aggrandizement. Call a spade a spade? Only when you are playing cards.

"I'll give him your card," Jack said, putting his hand out for a card, as though that would be an easy end to it.

"I don't have cards," I heard myself say, "that's for small-timers."

His eyebrows were on the rise again.

"Well, give me your name and office address, he'll have somebody check you out."

"I'm not a guy who sits in an office," I said, astonishing even myself with the dire depths of my deception. "Results is my middle name. And," I added with just the right touch of hauteur, "my phone is unlisted."

"So how do people get a hold of you?"

"They don't," I said. "I call them."

Now the dark eyebrows went whacko. "You don't know my boss," he said.

"And maybe I'd be just as well-off getting through life without knowing him."

He frowned and gave a curt nod that he must have thought was noncommittal.

"Tell you what," I said. "Let him know we talked. I'll call you in a couple days. If he's interested, I'll meet him." Then I added, unknowingly, the clincher: "By the way, I work like the ambulance-chasing lawyers: I don't find his daughter, I don't get paid."

A smile crossed his face, like a man realizing the razor being held at his neck was just for shaving. "He'll like that," he said, writing his phone number on a photocopy of a walking tour of the palms at Bernuli Junior College. "Sometimes he's so tight, he squeaks."

"She was anorexic," he said softly, a little ashamed. "Bulimic. I tried to help her. I couldn't do anything. I put

164

her in an institution. The best money could buy," he hastened to add, unnecessarily. He paused to control his breathing–to drain the flush from his face. "She escaped. Hasn't been seen since."

"How long ago?"

"Nine months or so."

"Been to the police? The FBI? Missing persons?"

He stared at me as though it were a naive question. "She's an adult. They seemed to spit on me. They went through some motions," he said. "Nothing came of it." Then he added, as though it surprised him, "I think they resented me."

"Why?"

"The way they acted. What do cops make now–twenty, thirty a year? Bound to be some resentment," he said, waving his hand to encompass his expensive property. "I never felt comfortable with them."

"Do you feel comfortable with me?"

He gave me the frozen fish eye. "I don't know yet."

"What is it you want? Just a notice that she is alive–or dead–or physical possession?"

He looked at me as though his nose were a gunsight. "Well, I would expect to see her," he said. "I mean, I don't doubt your integrity, but I'd have to have the physical evidence."

"Is it possible she won't want to see you?"

Darts came through the eyes. "Why would she not?" he faltered. I think I heard his voice break. "Of course...it's...possible." He put a spin on "possible," like anything was possible but he would just as soon not think it could be in this case. When he regained his composure, he asked, "So what would you charge?"

Here we were at the moment of truth. I had rehearsed my blasé response to this inevitable question in front of the bathroom mirror in our tract house. I had honed it to as near believable perfection as I was capable of bringing off. But now my tongue seemed to stick to my lower teeth. Michael Hadaad didn't let his gaze waver. Finally I shook my head, once. "Phew," I said with as much bravado as my thumping heart would allow. "Gonna be expensive."

"How expensive?" he asked, cocking an eye of suspicion.

"Not so simple," I said. "I bring her here and she's happy to come, I'd settle for two hundred."

"Two hundred dollars?" He thought he had gotten lucky.

"Two hundred thousand," I corrected him.

"Two..." he choked. "That's ridiculous!"

This is where my art came in. I nodded, the soul of understanding, and stood to leave. I nodded again, in acknowledgment of his hospitality, and said, "I quite understand. My fees are a lot higher than the run of the mill. There are many available for a lot less."

He just stared at me, as though I were the first person to ever walk out on him. For my part, I was not as bummed at the prospect of losing the case or the fee–it was a lark anyway–as I was of losing the opportunity to see his palm collection.

I turned to leave. I had not taken three steps when I heard the mighty Michael Hadaad say, "No, wait."

I smiled to myself before I turned. Now I cocked my eye–as he had done so expertly.

He answered: "You had the guts to get up. Most people can't see past their fee. Sit down."

I did.

"Is there room for negotiation?"

"I don't nickel and dime," I said. "I don't submit chits for meals and gas. But I'm afraid I've only given you the low side."

Up went the eyelids.

I nodded. God, I thought, is he buying this? But how could he? "If she doesn't want to come, it will be a half-million."

He sank back in his chair. I stood again, but faced him. "I quite understand your reluctance, Mr. Hadaad. I am used to working for the extremely wealthy, exclusively."

He waved me back into my seat, without looking.

Excerpts from *The Con*
A Gil Yates Private Investigator Novel
By Alistair Boyle

I have always had a soft spot in my heart for a con man. I'm not sure why. He is usually a man (sorry, ladies, most of them seem to be men) who makes his living outsmarting those who are smarter than he is.

He usually plays on the greed and the get-rich-without-working nature of people who have had more education and advantages than he had. People who should know better.

So looking for the most successful and most elusive con man was an assignment I couldn't resist.

The call came from the big man himself, Franklin d'Lacy. There was no baloney with an intermediary secretary. No executive wait while the honcho cleared his throat.

"Mr. Yates," he spoke clearly, distinctly into my voice mail at the phone company, with a clipped diction that put you in mind of the British Empire. It was only an affectation, though a very good one. "Your services have been recommended to me by a member of our board, and I would appreciate a return phone call at your earliest convenience."

d'Lacy was all smiles as he rose to greet me. "So good of you to come, Yates," he beamed. I could see in a flash why he was so good at raising bucks for his museum. (He always referred to it as "my museum". It didn't win him any extra friends.)

He was the quintessential salesman, but way too suave for used cars. High-end real estate, maybe, or mainframe computers.

He struck me as a guy sensitive of his height, but he wasn't that short. At five foot, eleven-some inches I was taller, but only by a couple of inches. He was dressed in one of those banker, pin-stripe, Brooks Brothers worsteds.

He was tan, had enough hair for the whole board of

directors and was fit as a cello. Did some jogging in the early morning to get the juices flowing, and after work a couple nights a week worked out those juices on a personal trainer of whom, it was said, he had carnal knowledge.

"Hold the calls, Miss Craig," he said, as the young woman backed out of the room. Do you suppose she sensed my predilection to stare at her sculptured buns? Everything here was a work of art—so much to stare at. The staff, I decided, was selected for their stare appeal, just like Hammurabi's nickels and dimes and Titian's oils.

So you could tell pin-stripe d'Lacy from your run-of-the-mill banker, he wore a gardenia in his jacket buttonhole. I could smell it from where I sat across his Brazilian rosewood desk, which was the genuine article, not the laminate, and was, roughly, the size of Brazil.

I couldn't get over how darn gracious he was. "Are you comfortable in that chair? May I get you something to drink?"

"Thanks, I'm fine."

"Well," he said, taking his measure of me down a nose that could have held its own with the marble statues in the foyer, "Michael Hadaad speaks very highly of you."

I almost fell off my chair. Michael Hadaad? The same guy who tried to clean out my sinuses with a bullet rather than turn over my fee after I had accomplished his goal? He was the last guy in the world I would expect to recommend me.

Michael Hadaad is my pseudonym for this slightly tarnished megabucks who put me through loops on my first case, from which I was grateful to escape with my skin.

d'Lacy seemed amused at my reaction. He was looking at me over the little temple he had made with his manicured fingertips. I could tell he wanted in the worst way to be British. It represented class to him.

"Michael is on our board, you know," he said.

"No, I..."

"Given us a nice piece of change over the years, I daresay."

I nodded. Why else would that creep be on

LAMMA's board of directors?

"Of course, he said you were a rank amateur. 'Childish,' was, I believe, the way he put it. 'A wimp, impossible to reason with'..."

"So why...?"

"Why is obvious, isn't it? You solved his problem. Look here, Yates, I'm a results-oriented guy. I wouldn't have made my museum a world-class institution if I hadn't been. Why, I'd work with a wooden-legged centipede if he brought me the pigeon."

Was there, I wondered, buried in there, flattery?

"He also told me the most remarkable thing about you," he said.

"Oh?"

Franklin d'Lacy nodded. "Said you worked exclusively on a contingency basis." He was especially amused when he said, "Michael quoted you as saying a thousand a day and expenses was tacky."

"Well, perhaps I..."

"That's what interests me," d'Lacy said. "That, and the fact that Michael assures me you are an absolute nut for privacy and secrecy. Discretion, he says, is your byword. No business cards, no office, not even," this he pronounced with relish, "a license."

Was Franklin d'Lacy really winking at me?

"Of course, I understand a contingency fee comes a lot higher than I could buy one of those small-timers, but if you achieve my goal, I will pay you one million dollars."

Also Available from Allen A. Knoll, Publishers
Books for Intelligent People Who Read for Fun

The Con: A Gil Yates Private Investigator Novel
By Alistair Boyle
Gil Yates is at it again—this time in the high-stakes art world, bringing the danger, romance and humor that Boyle's fans love. $19.95

The Missing Link: A Gil Yates Private Investigator novel
By Alistair Boyle
A desperate and ruthless father demands that Gil bring him his missing daughter. The game quickly turns deadly with each unburied secret, until Gil's own life hangs by a thread. $19.95

The Snatch
By David Champion
Two cops whose methods are polar opposites—in love with the same kidnapped woman—race against time and each other to save her. From Los Angeles' lowlands to its highest mountain, *The Snatch* races at breakneck speed to a crashing climax. $19.95

The Mountain Massacres: A Bomber Hanson Mystery
By David Champion
In this riveting, edge-of-your-seat suspense drama, world-famous attorney Bomber Hanson and his engaging son Tod explore perplexing and mysterious deaths in a remote mountain community. $14.95

Nobody Roots for Goliath: A Bomber Hanson Mystery
By David Champion
Mega-lawyer Bomber Hanson and his son Tod take on the big guns—the tobacco industry. Is it responsible for killing their client? $22.95

Order from your bookstore, library, or from Allen A. Knoll, Publishers at (800) 777-7623. Or send a check for the amount of the book, plus $3.00 shipping and handling for the first book, $1.50 for each additional book, (plus 7 ¼% tax for California residents) to: Allen A. Knoll, Publishers, 200 West Victoria Street, Santa Barbara, Ca 93101. Credit cards also accepted.
Please call if you have any questions (800) 777-7623.